A Christmas Tale
And Other Stories

Jan Weeks

This book is dedicated to all who believe that miracles are still possible, and that an open heart can overcome all obstacles.

Table of Contents

A CHRISTMAS TALE

The blizzard raged out of Canada on a blue norther, defying the meteorologist's prediction of a banana belt Christmas, not caring that I would be late for Christmas Eve, not caring that my children were expecting me, maybe. The Black Hills of South Dakota humped against the storm but the snow made its way through the thick stands of pines, howled down the channels carved by roads, filled every hollow and crevice with icy whiteness. *Only thirty more miles,* I prayed to whatever god might possibly be in charge today, *let me make it just thirty more miles.* However, that might require a miracle, and miracles don't happen to people like me.

I eased my car through the December darkness, peering into the dervish of snow that swirled across the secondary road leading to Rapid City and twinkling Christmas lights and presents and what was left of a once-familiar home. A headache built behind my eyes in inverse proportion to my creeping speed as I struggled to keep the car between the ditches.

My head whacked against the steering wheel as the car bounced off the road. Splinters of light spun in front of my eyes. I fell across

9

the seat, waiting for the whirling to stop. It took a couple of minutes to get my wits back. I scrabbled under the passenger's seat for my cell phone and punched the "talk" button. "No service" flashed across the screen. I opened the driver's door, pushing hard against tilted gravity, and got out.

Tentacles of hair whipped my face. My lungs burned from the frigid air. Snow filled my boot tops as I waded around the car, sending icy rivulets sneaking down my legs. By the time I'd plodded back to the driver's side, I knew I wasn't going anywhere anytime soon. I got back into the car, resigned myself to a long, cold night, and settled in to wait for morning. I'm a realist, if nothing else. In spite of the chill, I nodded off, vaguely remembering warnings about going to sleep and never waking up.

I woke, however, stiff and frozen. Wind still buffeted the forest, and snow had drifted over the car. I turned the key and flicked the wiper lever, listening to the blades grinding as they struggled to clear the windshield. Rubbing at the frost that had formed on the inside of the glass, I peered into the gloom. I blinked. Was that a light? I squinted and rubbed again. Two glowing squares shimmered through the storm.

The accumulated snow made the car door almost impossible to open, but I lay across the seat and kicked it until it gapped enough so I could squeeze out. Gravity slammed it shut. I pulled my coat collar higher and plunged through the hip-deep snow toward the lights.

A small log cabin nestled in the pines, half-buried by drifts. I guessed at where the steps might be and staggered up them. My foot caught on the top step and I flopped onto the porch. Gasping from the exertion, I managed to get to my feet and collapsed against the door.

It swung open almost immediately, and a man stepped back to let me flounder inside. The room spun as the heat hit me. Strong arms caught me as I staggered and carried me to an oversized couch. My vision blurred, but I saw a woman as she leaned over me and unbuttoned my coat. "My dear, whatever are you doing out on a terrible night like this? How long have you been out in this storm?"

I tried to slap her hands away and sit up, but the effort was too much.

The man—her husband, I assumed—tugged gently at her arm. "Let the child catch her breath before you give her the third degree."

"Put another log on the fire," she said, "and heat some water for tea." Then she bent over me again. "May I help you out of your coat and boots?"

I nodded and struggled to a semi-sitting position, shivering as she stripped my coat and boots off and rubbed my frozen feet between her warm, soft hands. Firelight struck sparks of silver in her hair as she helped me up from the couch and led me to a rocking chair in front of the fire. She wrapped a hand-knitted green and white afghan around me and propped my feet up on a stool.

"Now just relax." She bustled away.

I could hear the two of them murmuring in the kitchen, but my ears were as tired as my mind, and I didn't even try to decipher their words. Candles burned on the mantel, the windowsills, and the end tables, washing the log walls with a low, mellow sheen. It was a miracle that I'd been able to see the lighted windows through the storm. As warmth seeped into me, I began to drowse. Whatever tomorrow might bring, tonight I was safe and warm, and tea was on the way.

The rattle of china jolted me to full consciousness. The woman set a tray holding a teapot, cups, and a plate of cookies on a small table next to the rocker. She pulled the armchair closer and turned it to face me as her husband brought a wooden kitchen chair and settled down on the other side of me.

"Now, my dear, tell us your story," she said.

The last thing I wanted to talk about, especially to these Samaritans, was my miserable history. I put down my cup. "Excuse me. Where's the toilet?"

She pointed to the short hall that led to the bedroom. "On your left."

In the privacy of the bathroom, I stared into the flame of a pillar candle that burned on the vanity. I had about half a minute to think up some story, some lie, to tell this nice old couple. But my mind refused to produce a credible fantasy background. I used the toilet, then washed and dried my hands on the red and white striped towel hanging next to the sink.

I shuffled back to my rocker on feet that stung as sensation returned, hoping they'd forgotten the question. Fat chance. As I sat down, the man looked at me intently. "Now. What brought you out in a blizzard?"

I glanced from him to her. Their faces told me that only the truth would do.

"I'm on my way to Rapid City to spend Christmas with my—family." I took a sip of tea, a spicy, aromatic blend that was unfamiliar to me. "Unfortunately, God, or whoever's in charge up there—" I pointed upward— "decided my kids didn't really need good ol' Mom on Christmas Eve and shoved me into a ditch. I must have really pissed Him off and not even noticed." The man and woman frowned at my words, and I thought, *Uh-oh! A couple of goody-goodies.* I choked back an urge to let loose with a string of profanity, just

13

to see how they'd react.

The man spoke, his voice rumbling from a cavern somewhere deep in his chest. "God didn't shove your car into the ditch to punish you. That's what free will is about. We make choices, we live with the consequences of those choices."

Oh, yeah! Just what I needed. A preacher for a rescuer. I haven't really believed in a higher power since I was in high school and found out that you can do pretty much whatever you want as long as you don't get caught. And believe me, I've done it all. And spent a lot a time regretting and paying for the choices I've made. But I'd straightened my life out and things had been going pretty well, at least until tonight.

I thought of escaping to the car, away from these religious nuts. The wind howled around the eaves, snow scoured the window panes, and my toes and fingers tingled with warmth. I decided that listening to a sermon or two was a small price to pay for a night's comfort. Tomorrow could take care of itself.

"How many children do you have?" the woman asked.

Happy to be on familiar ground, I replied, "Two. Rory's five and Erica's three."

She lifted the pot and poured more tea into my cup. "I'm sure you'll be back with them soon. In a few days, they won't even remember that you were late getting home. Children are resilient, especially when they're loved." She gazed into the fire; a shadow darkened her eyes. But when she looked at me again, they twinkled.

I hoped she didn't notice me flinch. My kids barely know who Mom is, and that's probably a good thing. At least I spend a lot of time telling myself that.

"What about the rest of your family? Won't they be worried?" the man said.

I shook my head. "Don't really have a lot of family. Just my ex and the kids. And a couple of cousins I haven't seen since I was six."

The woman clucked her tongue. "That's a shame. It's so hard to be without loved ones, especially this holy time of year."

Oh, boy. This night was going to be a barrel of fun if the two of them were going to spend the night converting me. The storm wasn't looking so bad after all.

"Tell us about your little ones," she continued.

I shrugged. "They're little."

They stared, waiting for more. I almost laughed at their earnestness. I decided to shock these two pious people who believed all the bull of love and God and holy little Jesus. "I hardly see them. I live in Worland. They live in Rapid. Their dad has full custody and that's just peachy by me." I glowered at the man, daring him to say something righteous, but he sat silent. "I'm the world's lousiest mother, if you want to know the truth," I continued. "I didn't want kids in the first place, but when Jay and I got married, I was trying to live the American dream. Only, after a couple of years, I woke up. Dreams are for idiots."

I reached for a cookie, waiting for the old folks to jump down my throat like Jay, the cops, and the counselors had done for years. Hey, if the pros couldn't break me, these two geezers didn't have a chance. I could outlast anything they threw at me, and the worst that could happen was that they'd toss me back out into the storm. But somehow I didn't think they would, no matter what they thought of me.

"We had a boy once," the woman said. "The sweetest, most loving child you ever saw." The dusting of sorrow in her voice pierced the place where my heart had once been, and I blinked away the firelight that shimmered on my lashes.

"What happened?" I asked.

The man cleared his throat. "Nowadays I suppose you'd call it a hate crime, but back then, we weren't politically correct. He was different, and that made him a target. There was nothing we could do about it." He stared at his clasped hands. "It took him a long time to die."

Whoa! This was really more than I needed to know. I sneaked a look at the woman. Her face was serene in the firelight, her hands folded in her lap. I wondered how on earth she could hear him talk about her son being murdered and not want to rip her heart out. She smiled at her husband and he smiled back. Both of them looked so—so happy. It was unnatural. If anything happened to Rory or Erica, I'd probably kill myself. Even though I only saw them a few times a year, they were still my kids, and I loved them. I just knew that they were better off without me.

"They must be beautiful children," the woman said, "judging by their mother."

Oh, Jesus! Was I stranded with a couple of holy roller swingers? If either one of them made a move toward me, it'd be the last one they ever made. I stood up and set my cup on the tray. "Well, thanks for thawing me out."

"You're not thinking of leaving!" she said. "You wouldn't get half a mile in this storm. It would be a miracle if you even got back to your car."

"Yeah, and miracles are a little short in my life right now," I snapped. "Look, do you have a phone I can use?" I glanced around the cabin and saw a phone on the counter that separated the living room from the kitchen. I moved toward it.

"Storm took the power out," the man said. "Could be off for days."

I picked it up anyway. No dial tone. I was starting to have flashbacks to all the horror flicks I'd ever seen. If there was a chainsaw hidden under the kitchen sink, they wouldn't even have to fire it up. I'd die of a heart attack as soon as the old man hauled it out.

The woman came to stand by me. "You're afraid, aren't you?"

I could feel energy radiating from her.

"Wouldn't you be, in my shoes?"

She smiled and shook her head. "Perfect love casts out fear. We only want to help you through this trying time." She pointed to the couch. "Relax. Lie down. No one's going to hurt you, at least not tonight."

The candles burned steadily as the fire's heat swelled into the room. I looked deeply into her lovely eyes, and I knew she spoke the truth. Here, I was safe, from the outer storm and the inner one. Somehow I knew I'd never find such a haven again.

The man leaned back in his chair and crossed one leg over the other, ankle on knee. "God will never abandon you, though you seem to have given up on Him."

"See, that's the problem," I said. "Some old guy in a white robe, sitting on his heavenly throne, zapping sinners with lightning bolts. I just can't buy that horse

18

hockey."

He laughed, and it was as if all the cathedral bells on earth were ringing at once. "I think you've got God confused with Thor," he finally managed to say, "but you're wrong about Him." He sobered, and his expression became thoughtful. "You see, God isn't a guy. The scribes who wrote the Bible, and most of the other holy books, needed a way to describe Universal Wisdom, and since they lived in patriarchal societies, they naturally used the male pronoun. God is beyond sex. God is mother and father and all that is."

The room was silent as I tried to internalize that new thought. Suddenly, I had a vision of an eternal Couple, mother and father, holding hands and reaching out to take me into their embrace.

"That's right," the man said with a grin.

I stared at him, running a hand through my hair in exasperation. "How do you do that?"

The woman chuckled. "Honey, he does it to me all the time." She sat down in the rocker and put her feet up. I bypassed the couch and slouched in the armchair, my legs stretched out, elbows propped up on the arms, and my hands clasped on my chest. I hadn't felt this relaxed in years. Maybe never.

"We don't even know your name," the woman said.

"Sioux, like the tribe. God only knows

what my father and mother were thinking when they named me. I've always felt like I had to charge through life, being a warrior, in order to live up to it." My voice sounded bitter even to me.

"If you don't feel comfortable with it, why not change it? Names should reflect the inner person," the man agreed. "Now our boy—"

Her warning look silenced him. "She's not interested in ancient history." She turned to me. "Tell us about your parents, Sioux."

Somehow the words came easily, the words I'd kept inside for thirty years. I'd always said my life was nobody's business, but I *wanted* to tell this gentle woman everything, maybe because I knew she wouldn't judge me.

My voice felt like sandpaper in my throat. "They were a couple of drunks. And druggies. I left home when I was thirteen. Haven't seen them since. Don't want to." I waited for her shock, but her calm face showed interest, not disgust.

The man, too, listened intently, as if he were hearing my soul instead of my words.

"I bummed around for a few years, in and out of juvie lockup and detox. Did manage to finish school, though. Then I met my husband. Jay had a Jesus complex, I guess. Wanted to save the sinner, even when his folks threatened to disown him. Only it didn't work. Having two kids didn't help. So, being the

wise woman that I am, I gave them up to him."
I sighed. Now that I'd said them, the words
seemed trite and empty, not tough and
sensible. A tear escaped, hot on my cheek.

A log burned through and fell, sending a
shower of sparks up the chimney. The wind
wuthered around the cabin, moaning the storm's
name in a voice as deep as the old man's.

"I've really screwed up my life," I
whispered.

The man stood and laid a hand on my
shoulder. His eyes closed, and warmth flowed
through me. My body softened, and I wanted to
curl up in his arms and be safe and loved,
without judgment or fear. His wife's lips
moved but her murmured words were lost in the
sound of the storm.

"Rest now," he said. I stumbled to the
couch and was asleep almost as soon as she had
spread the afghan over me.

*****

The cold woke me. Dawn glimmered at the
windows, clear light glinting on the mounds of
snow that surrounded the cabin. I struggled
out of the afghan and stood up. The stillness
was absolute. I pulled on my boots and my
coat. They held lingering warmth from the
fire, now burned to embers. As the light grew
brighter, I noticed that last night's candles
had been put away, along with the teapot and
other dishes. I slipped down the hall to the

bathroom and was in full spate before I noticed that the towels and washcloths had vanished, along with the toilet paper. I reached under the vanity and found a roll. When I flushed, nothing happened. I turned the faucet to wash my hands, but nothing came out.

"Hey, what's going on?" I yelled. The silence was deeper than ever. I knocked on the bedroom door. It swung open. A bare mattress lay on the bed; the windows were shuttered. The stale smell of abandonment lay heavy. Where the hell were my happy hosts?

I rushed through the cabin again, looking for remnants of them, but it was as if last night had never happened. No water, no lights, no sign of the couple. My scalp prickled. People don't just disappear. They must have sneaked out while I was sleeping. I threw open the cabin door. The cold Christmas air filled my lungs and puffed out in tiny crystals. Deep snow filled the morning, trackless and white.

A rising red sun peeked through the pines, splashing the snow with rainbow-hued diamonds, and it was the most beautiful thing I'd ever seen. I oriented myself toward where I thought the car was and waded through the drifts, leaving a trail of blue shadows in the furrow that followed me. I did a good job of reckoning. In a few minutes, I saw the car sitting on the road shoulder. The windows had been swept clear, but there were no tracks anywhere near it. Bewildered, I got in. The key was still in the ignition. I turned it and the engine whirred, then throbbed quietly.

I put the car in gear, and as I gave it just a little gas to keep from spinning out, I realized that the old couple had never told me their names. They knew all there was to know about me, but they were as mystifying to me as all the spiritual stuff they'd spouted last night.

As I rolled down the road, on my way to Christmas with my kids, I wondered about God and ghosts and holy phenomena. I thought of my saviors, who seemed to love me in spite of my being me, and a mystical night in the middle of nowhere. Maybe miracles do happen, and maybe, just maybe, I am going home.

THE NIGHT VISITORS

Imagine a Christmas Eve, "soft" as the Irish say. Drizzle falls on palm trees and beaches. Los Angeles sparkles through the mist, Christmas lights as bright as neon on Sunset Strip. Cool enough for breath to gust out in silver plumes, but not cold enough to send cars skidding on ice-slicked highways and byways.

Imagine a church, brick and glass surging to the sky. A crèche, rich with gilt, greets worshipers, also rich with gilt. Plaster magi bear gifts, but their finery pales next to the clothing of those who parade past. Umbrellas jostle and bump as the media idols and icons approach the massive doors that swing open for the midnight service.

Inside, an organ thrums the air, sending a vibration into the soles and souls of pew dwellers. An air of expectation hangs over the sanctuary as over two thousand years of Christianity coalesce into celebration.

Imagine faces seen on the screen, both big and little. Faces that make the news and break the news. Children whose shoes could support a village in Zimbabwe if they were to be sold second-hand for a fraction of their original cost.

Now imagine that a man and a woman stand

at the curb, watching the movers and shakers file up the walk. Mist slicks their hair, haloes of damp against the Christmas lights. The man hunches in his not-so-clean fatigue jacket from a long-ago war. The woman, wrapped in a cloak made from an army blanket, draws her long skirt around her legs to hold what little warmth she can. Their eyes plead, their Styrofoam cups tremble as they silently ask for alms. A few coins thud into the used coffee containers, but no one meets their eyes. No one except a child.

"Daddy," Kristin whispers, "are they homeless?"

Her father pushes her gently. "I'm sure they have a home somewhere. Let's catch up with Allison."

The little girl skips ahead, heedless of the rain, and takes her sister's hand. "Should we invite them into the church?" she asks. "Maybe they'd like to hear the Christmas story and the music."

The fourteen-year-old glances over her shoulder at the beggars as she fingers a WWJD necklace made of Christmas-colored beads. All the girls in her clique at school wear them, a statement of fashion as much as of faith. "I'm sure they're not interested in Jesus. They ought to be in a shelter or someplace, not begging in front of a church."

Kristin looks back as Allison hustles her

through the door, reluctant to lose sight of the two strangers. Silver drops splash into puddles. The holiday lights blur in what has become a downpour. The strangers bow their heads against the wind. No star will shine tonight in the heavens over the City of Angels.

Kristin welcomes the warmth as she walks with her father and sister to their seat. The pews overflow with furs and silk and perfect coiffures. A thousand white tapers light the altar and twinkle from wrought-iron candelabra perched around the room. A hundred perfumes mingle with the pine scent from the massive evergreen that sparkles at one end of the chancel railing.

Kristin slips out of her coat, brushing the moisture away as she lays it over the back of the pew. "I have to go to the bathroom, Daddy," she whispers, and he nudges her on her way.

The tower clock signals the three-quarter hour, sounding like distant thunder as stragglers brush past the beggars, intent on arriving to worship the Christ. The sidewalk empties. The church doors swing finally shut. The man and woman stare long into each others' eyes, speaking silently of a celebration long past.

A gleam of light streaks across the church steps. Footsteps patter through the puddles. A small voice says, "You can come in if you want. It's warm in there."

Kristin takes the woman's hand and leads the couple into the church. They stop just inside the sanctuary. Kristin tugs on the woman's arm. The woman bends down to hear her whisper. "I'm sorry there aren't any seats left. But you can hear the music and get warm. I have to go back to Daddy." She smiles at them and hurries down the aisle. Her father frowns at her tardiness and damp hair, but the minister blows into the microphone and begins to speak before he can reprimand her.

"We have come to celebrate the birthday of Christ the Savior. Let us begin with a prayer," Reverend Halliwell intones.

Heads bow, hands clasp, and the service proceeds. The choir sings, the organ swells. Eyes fill with tears, emotion remembered from childhood, when people still knew Santa and Jesus and the angels intimately. Kristin turns toward the back of the church, beaming at the strangers who lean against the wall.

And finally: The music director steps forward, her voice spinning into the vaulted chamber. "As you know, our soloist passed on last week and we haven't had time to find another. As we sing our traditional closing piece, remember the voice of Mr. Dawes and imagine him singing the song he led for so many years."

The organ plays softly, andante, sixteen bars of ambiance leading the choir into the words: *Oh, holy night, the stars are brightly shining*.

Suddenly a tenor voice rises above the choristers. *It is the night of the dear Savior's birth.*

Heads turn, the organist falters as the words swell to the rafters, carrying the clarity of the purest bell in Christendom, the resonance of Moses on the Mount, the passion of a heart blessed. It is the voice of the beggar.

The raindrops in his hair catch the candlelight and reflect it toward heaven. The woman spreads her arms; the once drab blanket mimics the sky at dusk, sapphire fading to night. Their faces blaze as if Christmas has dawned in their souls.

Soprano blends with tenor as the choir stands silent: *Fall on your knees, oh, hear the angel voices.* The man sinks to one knee, facing God. Her cape surrounds his shoulders as she gazes down at him, her eyes filled with the love of a mother for her only child.

The minister stands mute, his jaw slack. The congregation turns as one and stares at the two singers.

Kristin kneels on the pew, watching the beggars, lit from within by a holiness born of innocence, one with the song. The man looks into her eyes as he sings the penultimate words: *Oh, night divine, oh, night when Christ was born.*

Their voices dwindle: *Oh, night divine.* The two strangers fold themselves into their wraps and disappear into the night. The door creaks closed behind them.

Kristin grasps her father's arm. "Did you see him?"

Stunned, he cannot speak.

Tears slip down Allison's face as she unclasps her necklace and drops it to the floor. She will never wear it again. She is too ashamed.

Reverend Halliwell's black robe stutters around him as he runs after the strangers, his purple stole askew. People push behind him; wonderment and suspicion tremble on their lips as they burst out into the rain.

The minister peers through the gloom, seeking the intruders, but the downpour blurs the world. The interlopers will forever be a mystery.

As the crowd turns to retrieve coats and purses, Kristin points to the crèche. "Look!"

Nestled next to the baby Jesus, are two Styrofoam cups, each holding a handful of coins.

MOTHER AND CHILD

The ornament nestled in excelsior, waiting. Christmas Eve was only hours away. The Elliott family would put up the Scotch pine that had been sitting in a bucket of water on the back porch for a week. They would weave twinkling lights through its branches and hang ornaments that spanned centuries, from the Bavarian emperor Maximilian I to the Victorian era, into the Great Depression, on to World War II, and those picked out at Target a few days ago. History documented in snowflakes, angels, and Father Christmases.

The ornament was the oldest of all, a wooden Madonna and Child, carved by a devout woodworker in Bavaria four hundred years ago. In the late eighteenth century, someone had tried to brighten up the dark wood with coats of bright red, blue, and gold paint. Now the paint was faded and worn. Only bits of blue remained on the Mother's cloak; a touch of red showed on Jesus's swaddling clothes. Golden halos had peeled and dimmed, leaving the baby Jesus almost uncrowned.

Three generations had passed since a wish had been made. The ornament waited for a child who still believed in magic.

*****

31

Beth Elliot plucked the ornament from its bed of plastic peanuts, dangling it by the frayed and tarnished gold cord. "Hey, Mom, where'd this come from?"

Be careful! Don't drop it." Eleanor Elliot snatched the Madonna and Child from her nine-year-old daughter's hand. "That belonged to Great-great-great-grandmother Elliot. I've managed to keep it off the tree for the last few years because your father would never forgive me if anything happened to it. Although why he wants to hang on to such a ratty little thing is beyond me."

Eleanor hung the faded ornament toward the back of the tree, as if she were ashamed to let visitors see them. The wooden figures seemed to disappear, eclipsed by shine and sparkle and twinkling lights.

Beth moved closer and peered between the branches. Mom was right; it was worn and peeling, but there was something about the baby Jesus and his mother that made her feel that being old and worn okay. Even without the bright paint, the woodworker's craft shone through, and the way that Mary looked at her child made Beth's heart feel funny. She wished her mom would look at her that way.

The front door burst open and a chill wind gusted through the house. Beth whirled around and sprinted to greet her father. "Daddy! Daddy!" As he swept her up in a bear hug, frost and aftershave mixed in her nostrils. She kissed his cheek, once and twice.

"Oof! You've gained sixteen pounds since this morning." He winked at her as he set her back on the floor.

"I have not! I hardly ate any lunch," she protested.

"That's because she ate half a dozen cookies as soon as they came out of the oven." Her mother came into the hallway, lifting her cheek for a peck from her husband. "Butter cookies, pecan bars, snickerdoodles, chocolate mountains—nothing was safe from our little Hoover."

Beth hung her head, her cheeks burning. Mom never let her forget that she was chubby. The slender, well-dressed woman wanted a daughter with a narrow waist, defined cheekbones, thighs that didn't rub themselves raw when she wore a skirt.

"Aw, leave her alone," Cameron Elliot said as he hung his coat in the hall closet. "Christmas only comes once a year. Just because you're always on a diet doesn't mean the rest of us have to be. And she'll grow into herself. Just give her time."

Eleanor's mouth turned down. "You'll be singing another tune when she has a prom date with a pizza instead of a boy." She turned and marched into the living room.

Daddy patted Beth's shoulder. "Don't worry, kiddo. Third grade is a long way from senior prom." He followed his wife, leaving Beth standing in the hallway.

Beth wished she could look the way her mom wanted her to, slim and trendy. But no matter what she ate—or didn't—her stomach bulged over her belt and her cheeks remained chubby. Mom didn't allow any junk food in the house; the Christmas cookies were for visitors. After tomorrow, the Elliots would be back to raw vegetables and rice cakes for snacks.

On the rare occasions that Daddy wanted dessert, they drove to the Baskin Robbins downtown, where he and Beth indulged in double-dip cones while Mom frowned at them from across the table. Beth envied the other kids in her class. They had ice cream at home. They brought candy bars in their lunch boxes. In spite of their sugar intake they weren't fat piggies, like she was. She wiped away a tear and went into the living room.

Daddy sat on the couch, sipping a bourbon and branch, as he called his evening cocktail. He circled one arm and Beth flopped down next to him, content to be held closely.

"We decorated the tree," she said, her sadness replaced by good humor as she gazed at it.

"And a darned fine job, too." Daddy lifted his glass in a toast to her and his wife.

34

"Now, I wonder what Santa will put under there for you?"

Beth laughed. "Oh, Daddy! You know there's no such person!"

Daddy's eyes widened as he looked at her. "Why, I know no such thing! In fact, I saw Santa just as I was leaving work, and he told me to tell you that you can expect a big, big surprise on Christmas morning. I think you'd better hang an extra-large stocking this year."

Beth burrowed into his chest. "You're so silly."

His hand was warm as he rubbed her back. "I guess Christmas does that to a person," he said gently.

*****

After dinner, a dozen couples stopped by for eggnog, cookies, and canapés. Lost in the grownup merriment, Beth was content to sit next to the tree, watching the tinsel sway as people walked past. The Madonna and Child hung within reach, and Beth stroked Jesus's face with one finger. "I wish I had your momma," she whispered. "She loved you so much. I wish my momma loved me. I wish I was thin, like her. I wish …." Her voice trailed away. Her yearnings were too huge, too secret to share, even with an old, wooden decoration.

Her mother's voice startled her from her reverie. "Time for bed. I'll come up in a bit

35

to tuck you in. Now say goodbye to our guests." Mom smiled at Beth, and Beth knew it was because they had company and because Mom had had two glasses of wine.

Beth rose and made her polite rounds, thanking the grownups for coming and wishing them a merry Christmas. Then she climbed the stairs and walked down the hall to her room. She put on her flannel pajamas and snuggled under the covers, taking up the book she was reading.

She was drowsing over the pages by the time Mom and Dad came up to tuck her in. Mom was still smiling. It must have been a good party. Mom bent over and took the book out Beth's hand. Beth roused. "Can't I just finish this chapter?"

"You're already half asleep. You can finish it up after we open presents in the morning."

Daddy bent to kiss her. "The sooner you sleep, the sooner Santa will come."

Beth threw her arms around his neck and pulled him close. "I love you," she whispered.

"And I love you, sweetheart." He hugged her back. "Sugarplum dreams and snow-white wishes."

He switched off the light, and Beth snuggled under the quilt. As she drifted to sleep, her last thought was of the wooden ornament.

*****

Hours later, Beth woke. The grandfather clock in the hall chimed twice. She slid out of bed and put on her fuzzy bunny slippers, then opened her door and peered into the hallway. A star-shaped nightlight dropped a pool of luminosity at the top of the stairs, throwing shadows down the stairwell. She crept down the hall and tiptoed downstairs. In the living room, moonlight sneaked in through a gap in the curtains and reflected from the tinsel on the tree. A gleam here, a shimmer there; the ornaments nestled among the branches. Packages filled the floor around the tree, mysterious shapes and sizes begging her to open them.

Beth couldn't remember ever seeing so many. She knelt down and studied the tags, looking for her name. She picked up a medium-sized box and shook it gently. Was it the chemistry set she'd begged for? Or could it be a bubble bath set? She put the box down and sat back on her heels.

In the branches, a light began to glow, brighter than any of the others. She inched around on her knees to see where it came from. Mary and Jesus hung there, surrounded by a soft golden light, seeming to be lit from within. Filled with wonder, she reached out.

As her fingers touched the ornament, warmth enveloped her, peaceful and loving,

37

like the feeling she had when Daddy snuggled with her. But this was like a hundred daddies all hugging her at once. Something rustled behind her. She turned slowly, somehow not afraid to see what might be there.

A boy stood in the middle of the room. His white robe shimmered against the darkness. Beth wondered how he had gotten through the snow in nothing but the robe and the sandals he wore. He must be frozen.

He smiled and she smiled back. "Hi," she whispered.

"Hello." His voice was like muted angel-song.

"How did you get in?"

He smiled and shook his head.

"Who are you?"

"I'm here to grant your wishes." He held out his hand. Beth's fingers tingled in his grasp. She stood up. They were the same height. He could have been one of her classmates if he hadn't been wearing such strange clothes.

"Do you trust me?" he asked.

She nodded.

The room dissolved around them. Beth thought she should be frightened but she wasn't. It seemed perfectly natural to be holding a strange boy's hand while floating down a golden tunnel. As she looked around, pictures began to form on the walls of the tunnel. Houses and streets and businesses appeared. As the walls grew brighter, Beth realized it was the town where her mother's parents, Grandma and Grandpa Stevens, lived. Their house appeared at the end of the tunnel.

As Beth and the boy shot out of the golden tube, the boy swooped onto the porch and through the front door, not bothering to open it first.

They floated through the living room to the dining room, where Grandma, Grandpa, and a girl about Beth's age sat at the dinner table. Grandma's dark hair gleamed in the afternoon light that shone through the windows. Grandpa's wrinkles had vanished, replaced by a smooth, tanned face. The girl had one elbow propped on the table, resting a chubby cheek on the heel of her hand. Though Beth had never seen a picture of her mother as a young girl, she knew the child must be her mother.

A platter of fried chicken sat in the middle of the table. A bowl of mashed potatoes was in danger of being bumped by Grandpa's elbow, while the gravy boat dripped cream gravy onto the hot pad. Green beans smothered in mushroom sauce snuggled next to a plate of steaming rolls.

A half-eaten drumstick lay across the girl's plate. Her eyes darted from Grandma to Grandpa as she pushed food around with her fork. If one of them looked at her, she took a tiny bite of beans. When they looked away, she went back to making designs in the mashed potatoes.

"Here you go, Ellie," Grandma said, passing her the plate of dinner rolls.

The girl straightened up and put her hands behind her back. "No, thank you."

Grandpa frowned at her. "One more won't kill you, honey. Don't hurt your mama's feelings."

The child took a roll and set it on her plate. As her parents watched, she slowly buttered the roll and took a bite. The grownups went back to their dinner and conversation, while the girl sat there, mute and miserable.

The boy led Beth to the window, and they sailed out into the evening sky. Darkness flickered, then brightness covered them again. The girl from the dinner table sat alone under a cottonwood tree in a schoolyard, swishing her hands through the leaves. The other children ran and screamed, happy to be free for a glorious fall afternoon recess. The girl looked longingly at her schoolmates, then stood up and brushed the leaves off her skirt, which stretched across her backside. She pulled at her blouse as she walked toward the school, trying to cover the bulge that crept over her waistband.

Five children spotted her and ran up to her, blocking her way. "Hey, Ellie-Belly. Where you goin'?" one girl shouted. The others roared with laughter.

"Just leave me alone!" the girl snapped as she tried to push past them.

A boy snickered. "Tubbo don't want us around."

The gang surrounded the girl. She tried to break through the circle, but her tormentors shoved her from one pair of hands to another, around the circle, chanting, "Ellie-Belly! Ellie-Belly! Nothin' there but lard and jelly!"

Tears streamed down Ellie's face. Her mouth distorted. She screamed, "Let me be! Please!"

The gang suddenly broke apart, running off in separate directions as the recess aide strode up to Ellie. "What's going on over here?"

The girl stood silent, staring at the ground.

"Were they teasing you? You can tell me. I'll see they're punished." The aide put a hand on the girl's shoulder, but Ellie shrugged it off.

"Well, if you don't want my help...." The aide scowled and walked away, leaving her standing there. The school bell rang, signaling the start of another long afternoon.

Beth stared at the boy, wanting to be certain. "Was that—my mama?"

His bright curls bounced as he nodded.

"But she's so thin now! How come she never told me she looked like me when she was little?"

Without speaking, the boy reached for her hand. The golden tunnel appeared and they streaked down it. Again pictures started to form.

Beth recognized her back yard. The snow had transformed into a carpet of green. A warm breeze rustled through the maple tree, and sparrows and finches darted from branch to branch. Her parents sat in lawn chairs, sipping iced tea while another Beth and two other girls shouted their way through a game of tag.

As the boy and Beth alit on the summer-warm grass, she thought she had never seen her mother look so relaxed.

"Beth's getting to be quite the little athlete," Eleanor said as she watched the children play.

Cameron nodded. "I told you to let her alone. She just needed to outgrow her baby fat."

Eleanor smiled at him. "You were right, of course. I just have a hard time forgiving my parents for overfeeding me. They laid such a guilt trip on me about eating Mom's good cooking that I felt I had to keep shoveling the food in, even when it made me sick. And then the kids at school were such beasts because I was fat. I didn't want that to happen to Beth."

He took her hand. "Ellie, you were never fat. Just plump, like Beth. You had to grow into yourself, too."

Eleanor slapped his arm lightly. "How would you know? We didn't meet until college."

"Oh, the family albums!" Cameron groaned. "You mom seems to forget that I've seen them five hundred times. She drags them out every time we go over."

"Exaggeration is the resort of a small mind." Eleanor chuckled, then sobered. "I'm glad Beth always finds better things to do than sit with the old folks and look at ancient photos. She thought I was a real meany for wanting her to slim down. But look at her now."

Cameron leaned over and kissed her on the cheek. "Since Beth shot up three inches, she's taken on a whole new shape. She's been doing a lot more this summer than sticking her head in a book all day."

"I think having some new friends has helped. It's hard to shed the image that people have of you. Almost as hard as it is to see yourself as you are, not as you were. And those inline skates you got her for her birthday were inspired."

Cameron nodded. "Only problem is that she wants me to join in."

"Well, why not? Maybe we can all go skating together."

Just then the other Beth ran up. "Mom, can Eva spend the night?"

As the scene began to fade, Beth noticed that her avatar seemed taller and thinner than she was. She wondered how old the other Beth was. But now she was streaking through the tunnel again, still holding the golden boy's hand.

More pictures, more lifetimes. The pictures flashing past slowed and Beth found herself standing in a large auditorium. A slender woman who looked to be in her mid-forties stood on the stage. The seats were full of people. The woman talked and the audience applauded. Beth and the boy floated in the wings, watching. The woman had dark hair like Beth's. Her chin and eyes were identical to Beth's. "Is that me?" she whispered.

The boy nodded. "Listen."

The woman's voice rose as if the boy had turned a radio knob. "Thanks to you and others like you, the Eleanor and Cameron Elliot Foundation has been able to build libraries in poor towns, not only in America, but in many foreign countries. We even have mobile libraries which utilize camels, yaks, and llamas to bring books to children and adults."

The woman waited for the cheers and applause to die down. "Ever since I was a kid, I've loved to read and loved to learn. With your support the foundation has been able to help others enjoy what I took for granted. I've been fortunate enough to travel around the world many times over, watching your dollars in action. Literacy flourishes where ignorance once prevailed. Children doomed to a life of poverty because they had no education have grown up to own and operate businesses, serve in civic capacities, and promote literacy themselves. We have given them books, taught them to read, and watched them blossom. There can be no greater reward. Thank you."

The woman stepped back from the podium as applause thundered through the auditorium. People stood, cheering and clapping, on and on.

The boy took Beth's hand and the vision began to fade as they entered the tunnel for the final time. In less than a breath, they were back in Beth's living room. Tinsel twinkled in the glow from the Madonna and Child as the ornament swung gently on its cord.

The boy gazed into Beth's eyes. "Do you understand?"

Beth faltered. "I—I think so. But can't you show me more?"

"I only show you what you wished for. Love and understanding. Loving yourself is as important as having someone else love you.'

Beth frowned. "Does that mean that Momma doesn't really love me?"

The boy shimmered. "If you were in danger, your mother would sacrifice herself to keep you from harm. But she's afraid, just as you were afraid. Show her your love, and it will be returned."

The glow around the boy began to grow fainter.

"Oh, please don't go!" Beth cried, reaching out.

But it was too late. She stood alone in the room. She turned slowly, gazing at the tree in wonder. Everything looked different, sharper, brighter, yet somehow softer, too.

She shuffled upstairs and climbed into bed. In a few hours she would wake again and go downstairs to discover what the wonderfully wrapped boxes held. She drifted off as the clock struck three.

*****

"Hey, sleepyhead," Daddy said as Beth wandered into the living room. The early sun slanted through the window, surrounding the Christmas tree with a halo of morning.

"Merry Christmas, Daddy. Where's Mama?"

46

"In the kitchen. Wanna open some presents?"

"In a minute." Beth skipped toward the kitchen, where bacon fried and the waffle iron heated. "Merry Christmas, Mama!" She threw her arms around her mother.

Eleanor smiled at Beth. "Merry Christmas. Would you like some orange juice?"

As Beth looked at her mother, glimpses of last night's travels flitted through her mind. She began to speak but closed her mouth; her mother would never believe her. "I love you, Mama. And I'm going to be just like you when I grow up."

Her mother held her close and stroked her hair. "Oh, you'll change your mind, I imagine. You'll want to be an astronaut or a doctor or a famous author instead of just a plain old housewife."

Beth looked up at her seriously. "I'm going to give books to children all over the world. But I'll still be just like you. Taking care of other people, keeping them safe."

Eleanor shook her head and smiled at her daughter. "What a strange, sweet child you are. Now let's get at those presents. I saw a lot with your name on them."

As the family dived into the pile of gifts, Eleanor reached for the mother-and-child ornament and unhooked it. "Cam, did you go on an art binge last night?"

"What do you mean?"

Beth stopped tearing Christmas paper to look as her mother held the ornament out to her father. Mary's robes were still faded, Jesus's blanket only a dim memory of red, but the haloes around the two heads shone with new gold.

As her parents puzzled over the change in the ornament, Beth's tummy tingled as memories of her magical journey replayed in her heart. It was going to be a great Christmas. It was going to be a great life.

MRS. EMORY'S CHRISTMAS

Mrs. Emory's Christmas lights drive me nuts. Ever since Tim and I moved next door to her three years ago, her twinkling red and green bulbs have blinked all night long. Who knew the little old lady next door would be, shall we say, eccentric? If I'd wanted to watch freakin' lights flash, we could have stayed in the city. God may have created light, but He sure didn't have twenty-four hours a day in mind, at least in suburbia.

As the lights burst into life at dusk one hot July night, sending Christmas-colored sparkles into our living room, I slammed shut the book I was reading. "I'm going over and tell her to turn the damned things off."

Tim, my husband, looked at me over the tops of his glasses. "She's a little old lady. Let her enjoy what few pleasures she has left." He's a real live-and-let-live kind of guy. I could see I'd get no help from him. So I muttered as I closed the drapes and grumbled my way back to my book.

Fortunately our bedroom's on the opposite side of the house from Mrs. Emory's lights. At least I can sleep without dreaming of elves and reindeer. Occasionally, when we have friends over for barbecue on the patio, her

Christmas lights blend with our Japanese lanterns and tiki torches, creating a certain ambience. Sometimes I see her curtains twitch when we're partying, and I wonder if we should have invited her over, but I don't think she'd fit in with soccer moms and stockbroker dads.

Mrs. Emory is older than God, or at least it seems like it. She tends her tiny garden in the summer, her wrinkled face hidden by an enormous straw hat, the kind my grandmother used to call a picture hat. It takes her forever to get from the back porch to the tiny plot where she grows tomatoes, bell peppers, and pole beans, with some marigolds and cosmos thrown in for fun. We nod and smile over the fence, if I happen to be mowing the lawn or playing with the kids (when they manage to pry themselves away from their video games) but we've never really spoken. I've also never seen Mr. Emory.

Emma and Sean, my little ones, like Mrs. Emory's lights. "Look, Mom. It's Christmas at her house all the time. How come it can't be Christmas here?" they whine. At the tender ages of four and seven, their "presents" sense is fully developed. Another thing to thank Mrs. Emory for: a reminder of the eternal search for stuff and more stuff.

On my more charitable days, I think that she's just trying to keep the Christmas spirit alive throughout the year, but those moments are few and far between. Call me Scrooge, but I believe in The Byrds or Ecclesiastes, whichever: To everything there is a season and a time to every purpose under heaven. And April and September aren't the seasons for Christmas lights.

Ours is a neighborhood of young people, wanting to raise their children in houses built in the era that spawned June Cleaver and Donna Reed. We want siding, not stucco; full-grown shade trees, not saplings; front porches, not arched entryways.

The average age is about forty, if you don't factor in Mrs. Emory. She's the only retired person within eight blocks in any direction. Most of the older folks moved out when Californians, Texans, and other transplants began to move in, but Mrs. Emory hung on to the family home.

Since we moved from Iowa to western Colorado, I can't really complain about the other "foreigners." Besides, the ones I know are good people. We all buy organic (whenever we can and if it's not too expensive), we trade play dates and recipes, and we live between the best elementary and the best middle school in the state, if standardized test results can be believed.

*****

Suzanne Taylor and I were having lunch at Il Bistro the Wednesday after Thanksgiving.

51

Suzanne's been in the neighborhood longer than anyone except Mrs. Emory. She's actually a Colorado native, but she's traveled. Her passport's filled with visa stamps from Europe, Asia, Canada, and South America. Suzanne expands my horizons. That's why I like to hang out with her. Of course, after a leisurely lunch, I usually go home depressed, wishing I'd been able to go and do and see the things she has. But really, I wouldn't change a thing about my life. Except the Christmas lights!

I vented to Suzanne over tiramisu and cappuccino. "I wish Tim and I had known about Mrs. Emory's holiday spirit before we bought our house. We would have looked for something a little farther away from Santa's Workshop South."

Suzanne took another bite of dessert. She never gains an ounce. Ticks me off. She finished chewing and said, "You don't know, then."

I hate it when she pulls that native stuff on me. My smile was as sweet as the dessert. "No, we've only been here three years, not forty-some."

She's only thirty-eight, but I had to take revenge for the calories that she doesn't absorb. Her frown told me she's ready for another Botox treatment.

She put down her spoon and looked at me in

52

a way that made me suddenly feel small and petty.

"What's to know?" I said, aiming for bravado but managing only to sound petulant.

Suzanne gazed out the window at the gray sky that threatened snow. Somehow she didn't seem to need that injection anymore.

"My mom went to school with Peter Emory, her son," she said. "People had barely heard of Viet Nam when he enlisted. We certainly learned about it when the local paper printed stories of his bravery. He seemed to have a sixth sense about danger that kept his squad from being decimated. We all thought his life was charmed." She looked at me, her eyes bright with emotion. "Then one day, his squad came back but he didn't. No one knew what happened to him. Officially he was listed as MIA.

"That was two days before Christmas, nineteen sixty-six. Mr. and Mrs. Emory swore that Peter would come home to Christmas, no matter when he came."

She sipped her cappuccino.

"And?" I prodded.

"The Christmas tree went out to the trash in May," she said. "Mr. Emory passed away without ever knowing what happened to his only child." The mist in her eyes trickled down one cheek.

By this time, I was tearing up myself.

"But that's over forty years ago." My voice broke and I cleared my throat.

Suzanne nodded. She didn't need to tell me that some things are not measured by calendars, but by the heart.

That night I told Tim what Suzanne said. "Aren't you glad you didn't go over and complain?" he said. I hate it when he's right.

The days inched toward Christmas, according to Emma and Sean. To me, they seemed like a swipe from a Brawny paper towel across a gloomy pane. In between wrapping presents in the wee hours and shoving them in the attic to keep them out of the reach of little hands, I baked double batches of everything. Mrs. Emory was flabbergasted when I showed up with the first plate of cookies. Twice a week I brought something to her, and she always thanked me so sweetly and offered to make some coffee to go with the pastries, if I'd only join her. But I always had an excuse: The kids were home alone; I had just run over for a minute; the next batch was in the oven and I had to get them out.

Before I knew it, Christmas was only three days away. I had just dropped off another plate of cookies to Mrs. Emory and run back home. As I opened our front door, I caught a glimpse of a dark blue car pulling into Mrs. Emory's drive. *Good,* I thought. *A little company for the old lady.*

That night, Tim and I lay in bed watching the local ten o'clock news. The plasma screen was filled with old file footage of jungles decimated by Agent Orange. Then a shot of helmeted soldiers with hard faces slogging through a river, rifles held above their heads. The commentator spoke solemnly. "The remains of a U.S. soldier were unearthed in the jungle fifty miles from Da Nang, Viet Nam, yesterday. Identification has been withheld, pending the notification of next of kin."

I slammed out of bed and ran through the house like a madwoman. I threw open the French doors to the patio and stared into the darkness. Mrs. Emory's Christmas lights no longer twinkled through the flakes that fell softly, gently, covering the earth like a shroud.

My bare feet tracked the snow as I ran to Mrs. Emory's house and rang the bell. I began to notice the cold as I hopped from one foot to another, waiting for her to answer. The plug for the Christmas lights tapped against the house, spinning in the bitter wind.

At last the door opened. Mrs. Emory still wore the clothes she'd worn earlier that day, an eon ago when I'd last brought cookies. Her eyes looked at me blankly; then her mouth curved upward just a tiny bit. "Come in," she said, stepping aside.

My wet feet tracked the carpet but we were

both beyond caring. This was the first time I'd been inside her home. In a corner of the living room, a table lamp cast a dim light that died in shadows as it tried to disperse the gloom. An armchair covered in doilies and antimacassars sat next to the table. Next to the chair towered a huge stack of presents wrapped in holiday paper, some faded, some new.

Mrs. Emory shuffled to the chair and dropped into it. Her hand fell to rest on the top package in the pile. Her lips trembled, and I crossed the room to kneel in front of her. "Was it—?" I struggled to remember her son's name.

"Peter will be coming home soon," she whispered. "Just not the way I hoped he would." Her tears fell like sleet, silver and cold, as I held her hand. I wanted to say something, anything, to help heal the hurt, but I felt like a child whose life experience ends at the back fence. Her empty world spread out before me, solemn and sacred, and the sight scared me. What if a half-grown Sean were called to a war half a world away? What if Emma didn't come home from school one day? My tears rose to join hers.

We sat that way for a long time, weeping without words, locked in sorrow. At last Mrs. Emory fumbled a tissue from the box beside her chair and handed it to me, then took one for herself. "I'm sorry," she said, her voice raspy.

"I'm sorry, too, for not knowing—or not caring, at least not enough," I said. "I wish I could have known your son. I wish he could have had just one more Christmas at home."

"I, too, wish—but there's no use in wishing," Mrs. Emory said. "Please let me fix you a cup of coffee."

"Don't trouble—" The look in her eyes silenced me. I helped her to her feet, willing to stay all night if I had to, to help this frail lady survive the blow she'd been dealt.

We turned to go into the kitchen when suddenly a strange glow shone through the windows, soft red and green. I went to the window and looked out and up, and—I swear to God!—saw every string of lights around the eaves burning through the veil of snow.

Mrs. Emory gasped. "I put the extension cord away this afternoon!"

I ran to the door and yanked it open. The plug still dangled free, swaying in the rising wind. Mrs. Emory put a hand on my arm and stared at the lights. As we watched, the bulbs blinked once, twice, three times. I looked at my neighbor. Her eyes shone as she stared at the lights, her hands clasped in front of her heart. I closed the door against the cold, and we slipped back to the window.

The lights blinked again, three times, and

then went out.

*****

Mrs. Emory moved into an assisted living home in April, and the lights came down. As her friends helped her to pack up her life in boxes and bags for the Goodwill, I went across the greening yard, carrying a plate of brownies. Mrs. Emory called a halt to the packing and poured coffee for everyone.

"I have something for you," she said, leading me to the garage. She handed me a bag marked "Fragile."

I knew what was in it even before I heard the bulbs clinking. I hugged my neighbor and whisked a tear away with my pinkie so she wouldn't see me cry.

She left that afternoon. A family with twin boys moved in less than a month later. I always planned to go visit her, but life got in the way. Then her obituary appeared in the paper, and I grieved for the time we didn't have.

I didn't attend her memorial service, but her red and green lights hang on the side of our house facing her old place. Every Christmas season they burn without flickering, lighting the winter nights.

SCARLET RIBBONS

Robert Trujillo hunched against the bitter wind that churned through the streets and tossed the falling snow in confetti madness. He shoved his hands deeper into the pockets of his worn denim jacket and wished he'd brought his muffler. He'd only walked six blocks, and his ears were frozen.

It was two days before Christmas, and he was on his way to the day labor office, hoping to pick up a job for the afternoon. Since the plant had closed six months ago, he'd floated from job to job, along with four hundred other laid-off employees. Too many workers, not enough jobs. His wife, Bonita, worked three nights a week at the local discount big box store, but her wages were barely enough to keep food on the table and pay rent.

They'd moved twice, each time to cheaper houses. Now their one-bedroom home was scarcely more than a shack. He hated that their son and daughter had to live like beggars. Leon was only four, but he was old enough to remember when he'd had his own room and new shoes when he needed them and something besides beans and rice and tortillas on the table. Luz, barely able to toddle, might forget this bad patch, if he could only

59

find another job, a full-time job. A job he could go to and hold his head up as he did a good day's work for a day's pay.

But right now, he'd take any job, any pay, to bring a bit of Christmas cheer to his family.

At the labor office, he stood in line for almost an hour before the sign went up: "No more jobs." Robert turned away, along with two dozen others who had not been lucky enough to find work. He pulled his collar higher around his ears and ducked out into the storm.

If the wind hadn't forced his head down, he wouldn't have seen the wallet. It lay, almost covered with snow, underneath the front bumper of a newer model car. He stooped to retrieve it and was just ready to stand up when a tiny mew caught his ear. A charcoal-colored kitten crept from under the car and looked up at him with amber eyes.

"*Hola!* Who are you?" he said, pocketing the wallet and reaching out for the tiny creature. "You're supposed to be inside, not out here in all this wet." The kitten seemed to agree with him as he lifted her and tucked her inside his jacket. Her little face peered at him, and he could feel her claws clinging to his blue sweatshirt.

A blast of snow blinded him for a moment. He bent over to protect the kitten as he jogged toward a nearby McDonald's. The heat almost overcame him as he pushed through the door. "Shh," he warned the kitten as he tucked her more firmly into his coat. "See the sign? No animals allowed." He fumbled in his jeans pocket for change and ordered a small coffee. He took the drink, which had reduced his disposable income to somewhere around three dollars, to a booth in the corner and sat down.

He laid the wallet in his lap and looked at it. Leather, monogrammed. No cheap Chinese junk. He looked around, then eased it open when no one appeared to be paying attention to him. Green peeked out at him. He fingered the bills; all hundreds, all crisp, enough to pay their rent for the next year!

The kitten nosed out of his jacket. "*Dios!* Look at all the money," he whispered, stroking her head with a finger. A purr answered him. He flipped through and found a driver's license. The man's name and face were unfamiliar to him, but the address was over in the ritzy part of town. "I keep this, our troubles are over," he muttered.

A claw dug into his chest.

"Hey! I'm the one who saved you, remember? Man, there's thousands in there."

His chest stung as the kitten stabbed its claws into him.

"Quit! He'll never miss it."

Ten claws penetrated his skin.

Robert thumped the kitten's head with his finger. "I told you to quit." He ran his fingers over the bills, feeling the richness of the paper. "Maybe he doesn't know how much he has here. If I kept just a couple—ouch!"

Robert jumped. The solemn face that huddled in his jacket watched him, eyes slitted.

He sighed and stroked the tiny head. "I know, I know. It ain't mine. I ain't gonna keep it, but can I at least look at it for a while?"

The cat purred and snuggled down against him.

Robert finished his coffee and tucked the wallet securely in his jacket. "Okay, *griego*. Let's go to Snob Hill."

*****

The house loomed through the storm, gray and imposing, three stories of stone and stucco. The kind of house Robert could come to only if he had a landscaping business name painted on the side of his truck. If he had a truck. For a moment, he hesitated. Surely the owner of such a home could spare a few hundred dollars.

A sharp jab from needle claws spurred him forward. He rang the bell; it echoed inside the house, seemingly forever. He shivered as he waited. At last the door opened and a stern-faced woman in a navy blue dress said,

62

"Yes?"

" 'Scuse me, ma'am. I got to see Mr. Hinkleman."

"I'm afraid he's busy right now. Come back later." She started to close the door, but Robert put out a hand to stay her.

"I got something belongs to him."

She held out a hand. "I'll see that he gets it."

"I give it only to Mr. Hinkleman," Robert insisted, moving back a step.

The woman stared at him for a moment. "All right." She stood aside and let him in, closing the door against the swirling snow. "Don't move from the mat." She tapped away on sensible heels as Robert reveled in the warmth of the great entryway. In a few minutes, he heard a man's steps, and the wallet's owner appeared.

"You have something for me?" Mr. Hinkleman looked doubtful.

Robert held out the wallet. Mr. Hinkleman paled as his hand went to his back pocket. "Oh, my God!" he yelped. "Where did you find it?"

"Under a car on Spruce Street."

Mr. Hinkleman grabbed the wallet and thumbed through it, counting the money. He was too well-bred to sigh with relief but Robert saw it flood over him. "Thank you, Mr.—uh ...."

"Trujillo. Robert Trujillo."

63

Mr. Hinkleman dug in his pants pocket and came up with a folded sheaf of bills. He peeled off the top one and handed it to Robert. "Thank you for returning my property, Mr. Trujillo. Have a nice Christmas."

"Thank you, sir."

Hinkleman opened the door, and Robert knew he was dismissed. He nodded to the man and walked out into the storm. The door closed behind him. In the fading light, he examined the bill. "Man, I hope he don't lose no sleep over his generosity," he mumbled as he stuffed the twenty into his jeans pocket.

Half an hour later he was nearing home. The superette on the corner was still open, and he went in. He couldn't very well toss the kitten back into the storm, but their household didn't have the necessaries: cat litter, cat food. He took a cart and wended his way through the aisles, choosing the cheapest bag of dry cat food and a small bag of kitty litter. Those two things took almost half of the twenty.

"Oh, what the hell! It's Christmas." He reached into the cooler case and took out a six-pack of Miller High Life, the cheapest beer they had. He added a gallon of milk and two packs of Twinkies for the kids to the cart. He stuffed the two dollars the clerk handed him into his jeans pocket and hefted the bags. "You're gonna have to hold on by yourself," he said. The kitten hooked all four feet into his sweatshirt and settled in for the ride.

Leon and Luz scrambled to meet him as he entered the house. "Papa! Papa!" Leon shouted. "What did you bring us?"

Robert laughed. "Close your eyes and hold out your hands."

Leon hurried to obey. Luz copied him. Robert laid the kitten in his son's hands. "Careful now. Don't squeeze it. It's your Christmas present."

Leon's face lit up as he gazed at the scrawny cat. Luz waddled to Leon and held out her pudgy hands. "C'is'us!" she cried, mangling "Christmas" all to hell.

And so the little gray cat became Kisses.

Bonita was predictably put out. As she and Robert retired to the kitchen, leaving the kids in the living room with the cat, she hissed, "What were you thinking? We can't even feed ourselves, and you drag home another mouth! Why didn't you get the kids something besides junk food?"

Robert popped the pull tab on a beer and raised it toward her. "How many beans can *niños* eat? They need something for the joy as well as for the stomach. Did you see their faces when they saw *el gato*? Their hearts are fed, too."

Bonita's scowl softened. "And beer. What

good is beer?"

He caressed the nape of her neck, loving the feel of her silky hair on his arm. "Is good for us *viejos* to have a little joy, too."

She swatted at his hand, but her smile told him he was forgiven. "I'll get the glasses."

Robert grinned and took another beer from the pack. She brought the glasses and poured the beer. They sat down at the table. Robert raised his glass. "To a merry Christmas and a prosperous new year!"

"From your mouth to God's ears," Bonita said, clinking her glass against his.

As they sipped, he told her the story of the wallet. "You should have kept the money," she said, after hearing of his reward. "A rich man like that? He'd never miss it."

Robert looked deeply into her eyes. She dropped hers first.

"Your mama would not like you to marry a thief. We can sleep tonight, but will Mr. Hinkleman?"

Bonita covered his hand with hers. "Merry Christmas, *mi amor.*"

*****

The next day the blizzard abated, leaving two feet of snow on the flat and drifts as high as a man's head. Robert shoveled their walk and started knocking on doors, hoping to pick up pocket money. By the end of a back-breaking day, he'd garnered almost a hundred dollars.

The light was fading as he slogged up the steps of the stoop. He stamped his feet clean of snow and went inside. Luz and Leon snuggled on the couch, petting and laughing at a purring Kisses as Bonita slipped her company tunic over her head.

Robert kissed her and handed her his earnings. "Here, honey. Get the kids some toys tonight."

She looked at the wad of bills and gasped. "Christmas after all! I'll get a chicken and tortillas, and some lovely fresh vegetables. We'll have a real dinner tomorrow!"

"Don't forget the toys."

Bonita chewed her lip. "We could stock the cupboards—"

"Toys!" Robert touched her cheek. "Children need fun, too."

She leaned into his touch. "Whatever I can carry on the bus. Meet me at the stop? I'm off at eleven."

*****

"Papa, will Santa find us?" Leon asked, his little face serious.

Robert tousled his hair. "Santa always knows where to find good children. He will find you. This I believe." He was glad that there would be some presents, some candy, perhaps stockings for the little ones. With

67

the big discounts the store always gave on Christmas Eve, Bonita should be able to bring his son and daughter at least some of the things they had asked Santa for when he'd taken them to the mall a few weeks ago. Too bad about the tree, but no way could they afford one, or the decorations to put on it. Even a short, scrawny spruce cost over thirty dollars.

"Now you must go to bed, or Santa will not come," he said as he lifted Luz into the air.

"Kisses!" she cried, reaching for the gray kitten who batted at a string Leon was dragging across the floor.

"Yes, Kisses will sleep with you," Robert assured her. "Now, off to bed!"

"Sing us a song, Papa," Leon begged.

"Okay. But only one."

"The ribbon song!" Leon's eyes sparkled.

" 'Ibbon," Luz mimicked.

Robert tucked the children into the bed they shared and sat on the edge. His true tenor touched the words of a song he'd learned long ago, a song of magic and love and a father's quest to fulfill his daughter's prayer. Of a midnight search through empty streets, a futile search for scarlet ribbons. Of the miracle of finding the ribbons in the dawn, laid out on his sleeping child's bed. By the time he'd reached the last line, his children's eyes had closed, and he whispered the last line. "If I live to be a hundred, I will never know from where came those ribbons, lovely ribbons, scarlet ribbons for her hair."

He stroked Kisses, who lay between the sleeping children. "*Buenos noches, griego*. Too bad there's no more magic in the world."

*****

At eleven-fifteen, he peered into the children's room. They were nestled together; Kisses snuggled between them on the pillow. Amber eyes stared at him. "Watch them, *griego*. I'll be back in a few minutes."

Robert put on his jacket and slipped out the front door into the frosty night. He locked the door and trotted off to meet Bonita's bus, the last one of the evening. Stars hung low over the street, brilliant in the midnight-dipped sky. He breathed deeply. A bell tolled from the Catholic church a few blocks away. He wished he could detour and kneel in the incense-filled candlelight and pray for his family, himself, and all those around him. But the children couldn't be left alone too long. And Bonita was waiting.

*****

They walked through the night, breathing mist out as they talked. Robert carried two bags filled with food. Bonita carried one, from which the head of a teddy bear peeked. "Leon needed new pants. I hope he's not too disappointed that Santa brought him clothes," she said with a sigh.

"He'll love the motorcycle set," Robert said. "He has never had three motorcycles at once. And Luz practically demanded a purple bear when she saw Santa at the mall."

"At least they'll have something," Bonita replied.

As they turned up the sidewalk to their front door, Bonita stopped short. "What on earth?" Packages, bags, and bundles lay on the stoop.

Robert dropped the sacks he was carrying and vaulted over the pile. He fumbled the key into the door and burst inside. "Leon! Luz!" he shouted as he raced to the bedroom. Two heads stirred under the blankets. Kisses watched him with sleepy amber eyes. He slumped against the door jamb. *"Gracias a dios,"* he whispered as he turned back to the front door.

Bonita had managed to pick her way inside. She dropped her sacks on the couch and murmured, "Robert. Help me get these things into the house."

"It's a mistake," he muttered as he began hauling bundles and boxes inside.

"No mistake," Bonita said, emptying a bag and examining the tags on the wrapped presents it held. "Look. 'Leon.' 'Luz.' These are meant for us."

They brought the rest inside and closed the door against the biting cold. As they went through the bounty, they discovered presents for themselves, too. One box held Christmas lights and ornaments. "What good are these without a tree?" Bonita wondered.

Robert opened the door and peered around. In the shadows off to the side of the stoop, he spied a fir tree, cut and nailed to a wooden stand. He dragged the tree into the house. The smell of Christmas filled the room.

"I don't understand," Bonita said.

"I think I do." Robert's lips twisted in a smile. "Mr. Hinkleman. He must have had a change of heart. Decided twenty dollars wasn't enough reward for returning his wallet. He sent all this."

"But how did he know where we live? And our children's names?"

Robert scratched his head. "A rich man has ways of finding out anything. And tomorrow I will go and thank him."

*****

Leon's screams woke Robert. "Papa! Santa came!" Robert rolled off the Hide-a-Bed that he and Bonita shared in the living room and grinned at his son's awestruck expression.

"Of course, he came. Did you think he wouldn't?"

Leon turned a serious face toward him. "I— I wasn't sure, Papa."

Bonita sat up and pushed the hair from her face. "Wake your sister. Then find the

71

presents with your name on them."

Leon scampered back to the bedroom and in a moment hustled a groggy Luz into the living room. Kisses strolled behind them. And joy reigned.

*****

As the sun swung westward toward a hazy horizon, Robert walked briskly up the walk to Mr. Hinkleman's house. He rang the bell and waited. He was ready to turn away when the door swung open and the woman, dressed in jeans and a sweater instead of a dress, eyed him sternly. "Yes?"

"I would like to speak to Mr. Hinkleman."

"Impossible." She started to close the door.

"Please! I have to thank him!"

The door swung open again. "For what?" she said.

"For the presents, the tree. For my children's Christmas."

The housekeeper looked at him as though she were contemplating calling the police or the asylum. "You're mistaken."

"No. He sent us toys, food, even a tree. My wife and I found them when she got off work last night, piled on the porch."

The woman looked puzzled. "I can assure you that Mr. Hinkleman was not responsible for any of that."

Robert raised his brows. "How do you know

he didn't?"

She looked him in the eye. "I carry out all of his instructions, and he did not give me any regarding you or your children. Mr. Hinkleman is not a charitable man."

"But we have the gifts."

"Someone else is responsible."

Robert stiffened. The woman didn't know everything, even though she acted like she did. "You're wrong," he blurted.

Her look was cold. "I will tolerate your rudeness only because you don't know any better. Mr. Hinkleman is not your benefactor. He left for Grand Cayman Island two hours after you returned his wallet." She closed the door, just short of a slam.

Robert made his way toward home, oblivious to his surroundings until he was walking up the steps to his front door. He shut the door behind him and looked at his children, playing with their toys. Delicious smells drifted from the kitchen.

As he sat on the couch, something crackled. He rolled onto one buttock and felt around. He pulled out an envelope. An envelope with his name on it. No address. He ran a fingernail under the flap and took out the paper inside.

We are happy to say that the Pierson Tool and Die Company is reorganizing and hiring for all shifts. Please report to the main office on Tuesday, December 28th, for an interview.

"Bonita!" he cried, springing to his feet. "The factory is open again! I have to go on Tuesday for an interview."

His wife came out of the kitchen, wiping her hands on her apron. "What did you say?"

"I'm going back to work!" He grabbed her and swung her off her feet, laughing like a *lunático.* He showed her the letter.

Tears fell as she read it. She handed it back. "I must finish cooking dinner. We have much to celebrate, *mi corazon.*"

The events of the last couple of days overwhelmed him; he sank onto the couch. Kisses padded across the floor and leapt into his lap. The cat blinked its yellow eyes as its tiny paws kneaded his belly. He stroked the little creature and whispered. "Perhaps you brought us luck. Or perhaps...." Robert looked heavenward. "Perhaps God still hands out miracles, eh, *griego*?"

A contented purr was his only answer.

A SCENT OF SNOW

I envy the lives lived behind lamplit curtains. In autumn and winter I stroll at dusk, watching shadows move across lace or brocade, safe and warm and ready to sit down to a cloth-covered table and share the day with each other. I imagine the inhabitants retiring to the living room, dishes magically back in the cupboards without a wet hand in sight, where they sit listening to music by Haydn or 101 Strings, curled up on overstuffed sofas and chairs to read or talk or simply snuggle up until bedtime.

I live alone. The house doesn't get cleaned unless I haul out the mops and dust cloths. I don't eat unless I shop and cook and wash and stow in cupboards. I live with second-hand furniture, worn and lumpy, marred and scarred, rather like me. Have I picked my surroundings to fit my life? Or have I shaped my life around these cast-offs? If I wander through dark streets long enough, maybe I'll find the answers.

Christmas this year sneaked up, almost without warning. I rely on the weather to alert me to holidays but this fall had been too balmy, too soft to bring in "the holiday season." The only reason I knew Thanksgiving had rolled around was that I didn't have to go to my job as a legal secretary for four days. Without relatives, with few friends (and those already promised to others) I spent the day alone, eating yogurt for breakfast, a roasted chicken leg quarter and instant mashed potatoes with packaged gravy for dinner. I didn't bother with supper. A chunk of bleu cheese, butter crackers, and a bottle of merlot sufficed. The television absorbed me all evening with the first rerun of *It's a Wonderful Life.* No matter how many times I watch Jimmy Stewart plunge off the bridge, chills still run up my spine, and I wish for my own angel. Alas, Clarences do not make appearances in my town. Unfortunately, the angels that hover around my life already have their wings, and they're much too busy to bother with a middle-aged woman who has surrendered her dreams to Fate.

And so Christmas crept in on ice-free breezes, frosted occasionally by morning hoar that vanished by nine. Skies curved blue above high-rises and four-lanes, cropped fields and browning grass. The last scarlet and gold leaves dangled, crisp and lonely, from limbs that basked in warmth that belonged to September.

"Sure is crappy weather for Christmas," Caralee, the law firm's bookkeeper, muttered. "My kids are wild. 'How is Santa going to drive his sled with no snow?' 'I wanna go ice skating. How come the pond's still wet?' As if I have the answers to life's questions," she finished, scowling.

I kept my eyes on my monitor and my fingers clacking. I try not to fraternize, even though Caralee wants to be bosom buddies. I've never had children and thank God every day for that. So women who chatter on about their little darlings bore me senseless.

Unfortunately, most people bore me. Or frighten me. Even Mr. Taylor, Mr. Sanderson, and Ms. Lee send me into tizzies whenever they venture beyond the bounds of duty and inquire into my life. I feel that my responsibility is to show up on time, work industriously and efficiently, and keep my life to myself. After five years, I think they're finally getting it. At least they don't indulge in company picnics, although they host an obligatory Christmas party. I always go, stay for half an hour, sipping the one glass of red wine I allow myself at these functions and nibbling half a dozen catered canapés. I'm always glad to leave.

Esteemed clients are also invited, along with the help, and they bring husbands and wives and other esteemed (read big-shot) potential clients. I can usually find a chair in a corner where no one will bother me as I do my dutiful best to show I'm loyal to the firm just by showing up.

This year I treated myself to a new forest green velvet cocktail dress, in honor of the bonus the company handed out. The sleeves skimmed my wrists, bell-like, my hands the clappers. The neckline scooped a little lower than I liked, but I folded and pinned the cups of my Maidenform so that my bra didn't show. The skirt fell just below my knees, draping into folds that swirled when I walked. I felt extremely elegant as I tottered from my bedroom to the living room on the one pair of stiletto heels I own. By the time I'd paced the length of the living room a dozen times, I'd regained my sea legs and could walk without wobbling.

For one insane moment I wished I'd kept Great-aunt Dora's mink jacket that she'd bequeathed to me, but the money I got from selling it to a local furrier had fattened my 401(k) by several thousand dollars. So I wore my black wool coat, the only winter coat I had. The people at the office had seen it a thousand times. With luck they wouldn't notice it any more than they noticed the wallpaper in the reception area.

As I drove to the party, I passed a shop that was still open. The window held poinsettia bouquets, pine and tinsel garlands, and Christmas-themed corsages. On impulse, I pulled into a vacant parking spot and walked back to the shop. As I entered, a bell attached to the door tinkled and the scent of hothouse flowers enveloped me in false spring.

An elderly man rose up from behind the counter. I started. I'd expected a clerk to come from the back room, and I'd expected a woman. A man in a flower shop seemed to be an oddity. Without speaking he went to a cooler, slid the door open, and took out a fiery red blossom surrounded by gold and silver ribbons.

Still without speaking, he brought it over to me. "For your special night," he said as he pinned it to my coat. His accent was European; German, I guessed.

"Wait a second. How do you know I want this?" I reached to unpin the corsage. His withered fingers stopped mine. His skin was as soft as watered silk, warm as a summer midnight.

"Of course you want it. That is why you stopped, *nicht wahr*?"

I opened my mouth to contradict him, but no words came.

He smiled a beatific smile. "Now go. I have to lock up." He took my arm and steered me toward the door, firmly but not unkindly. I fancied I felt the warmth of his hand through wool and velvet. "Put the flower on your dress when you arrive," he instructed as he opened the door. The bell tinkled and I found myself on the sidewalk.

"But how much—"

The door shut behind me and the old man pulled down an old-fashioned roller shade. Before I could raise my hand to knock and get him to open up so I could pay him, the shop went dark.

As I walked to my car, my nose picked up the flower's fragrance, sweet but subdued. Then a cold smell swept over the city, a disturbing scent of storm and snow. I looked up at the first stars sparkling in thin cobalt twilight, but even as I looked, pewter clouds streamed in from the west, snuffing the sky. I was glad to get into my car.

Full dark had fallen by the time I drove up to Mr. Taylor's house. His circular drive was lined with cars. Windows shone in the three-story brick home and electric candles gleamed on window sills. No flashing icicle lights or nodding reindeer on the lawn. Mr. Taylor liked his holidays restrained, just like he was.

I stopped at the door. A uniformed valet pranced out to take my keys and give me a chit. "Have a nice party," he said as he helped me out of the car.

"Thank you." I pulled my coat closer against a vagrant breeze and walked up the sidewalk to the door, which opened magically. A butler, rented for the occasion, bade me welcome and grasped the collar of my coat as I slipped out of it.

"Would Madam like to wear her corsage?" he asked, speaking above the sounds of merriment coming from deeper inside the house. When I nodded, he unpinned it and laid the coat on a side table while he fastened the flower to my left shoulder. He bowed me on my way and disappeared with my coat.

I took a deep breath and walked toward the festivities, taking confidence from the velvet swirling around my calves and the gentle fragrance from my corsage. The smell hovered between passion and peace, faint but pervasive. I wondered what kind of flower it was.

The arched entry into the living room had been lined with sweeping pine and ribbon garlands. White candles of all sizes burned on the mantel and reflected from an ornate mirror the size of my bathroom, creating a sophisticated ambience. I scanned the room, looking for the most remote unoccupied chair, and spotted a tartan-covered wing chair in the far corner beside the fireplace.

A waiter approached, his tray filled with crystal wine glasses, glittering in ruby and pale lemon and champagne. I took a glass of deep burgundy, smiled my thanks and began a circuit of the room, which would take me to each of the firm's principals for a holiday greeting, then bring me to my tartan

81

sanctuary.

Mr. Taylor, flushed with heat and whiskey, clapped me on the shoulder. "Glad you could make it, Joan."

"Thank you for inviting me," I replied.

"Make yourself at home," he said, gesturing with his drink.

I murmured something innocuous and began my slow promenade to the next partner. As I made the rounds, I kept an eye on my refuge. Still empty, thank goodness. Once I got there, the evening would be bearable. It took me twenty minutes to circle the room, nodding and smiling and generally feeling foolish. Did I mention I'm not good at crowds?

Finally I'd made contact with the last of the partners and started toward my haven. Damn! A tall young man had usurped my seat. Now I'd have to find another hiding place. I scowled at him, hoping my ill will would shift him but he didn't seem to feel my animosity. Perhaps that's too strong a word. The scent of my corsage drifted to me, enclosing me in a dreamy goodwill toward men. After all, it was just a chair.

The man looked up and our eyes met. I felt a quiver in the pit of my stomach, like a recognition of a fellow soul. Out of habit, I clamped down on the feeling. No point in getting giddy about someone I'd never see again.

But I wasn't going to give up my chair meekly. I sidled through the crowd, keeping my expression impassive. As I approached, the man stood. He was taller than I'd thought, over six feet. "Hello. My name's William Turner," he said, holding out his hand.

I automatically took it. "I'm Joan Dalrymple."

"Nice to meet you, Joan." He gestured toward the chair. "Would you like to sit down?"

I ignored his gesture. If I sat he would tower over me like a pine tree over a holly bush.

"That's a lovely corsage you're wearing." William leaned closer. The flower scent grew stronger, seeming to envelop us both in its mysterious fragrance. Happiness swept over me. I began to enjoy the party, or at least my little corner of it.

"There you are!" Mrs. Taylor's cry rose above the noise of the party. "I haven't seen you since last Christmas, Joan," she laid a hand on my arm. "I'm so glad you could make it."

"I'm glad to be here," I said.

"I see you've met William," she went on. "Will, dear, what do you think of our Joanie?"

Our Joanie? Nobody ever called me that.

Will smiled down at me. "She's lovely. I'm so glad you invited her."

83

Dazzled, I smiled back.

"Oh, Ted couldn't get along without her," Mrs. Taylor went on. "He says she runs the office. He just shows up to take care of the minor matters." Her laugh tinkled through the hubbub.

I stood stunned. What had possessed her to say such a thing? The flower scent grew, spreading around me.

"What a lovely corsage," Mrs. Taylor said. "Wherever did you get it?"

Before I could answer, Ms. Lee, the junior partner in the firm, came up. "Hello, Joan. Glad you could make it." She raised her champagne glass in salute. Suddenly my little corner of the party was getting crowded. "Hi, Will," she went on. "I see you've met Joan. Isn't she a marvel?"

Will raised an eyebrow at me. "I haven't had a chance to find out," he said, grinning, "but I'm sure I will. I really want to."

A blush crept up my neck and warmed my cheeks. "You'll all have me stuttering next," I managed to say.

"Come," Mrs. Taylor said. "Let me introduce you to some people." She put a hand on my arm and drew me away from William and Ms. Lee. I spent almost an hour mingling and chatting and exercising social skills I hadn't been called on to use in years. Almost every person commented on the corsage the old man had given me. I noticed that instead of drooping in the heat, it seemed fresher than ever. Its scent filled the room, subtle but overlaying the smells of food, candle wax, and a cigarette or two.

Then William was at my elbow. "May I steal away your protégé?" he said to Mrs. Taylor.

"Of course, Will." She smiled at us like a satisfied mother whose daughter is headed off to her first prom.

I felt the warmth of his hand through my sleeve as he led me toward the patio. The French doors stood ajar, letting the impression of impending snow into the room, alleviating the heat generated by a hundred or more bodies. We stepped out onto cold flagstone. The clouds reflected the city lights, reflecting a pink luminosity over us. The scent of snow was strong. I shivered.

William put his arm around my shoulder "Breathe that in," he said. "The freshness of winter. The Druids and many other ancient peoples celebrated Yule as the time of death and resurrection. As the sun died through the autumn they stockpiled presents for the gods or god so they could bring the sun back on December twenty-second."

"And the cycle began again." A stray flake touched my cheek.

"So, Joan. Tell me about yourself." Will smiled down at me.

I looked toward the city. "I'm a legal secretary."

"I sense hidden depths that don't fall under that job description," he said.

I drew away, folding my arms over my chest against the shivering that had begun. "Nothing hidden here."

"Oh, but everyone has a secret." He stepped closer.

The fragrance of the corsage intensified, blotting out the crisp odor of night. Dizziness staggered me, and I put out a hand to steady myself. The night faded to black.

* * * * *

A spring wind blew around me, carrying bits of paper and dust along with a hint of lilac. The sun told me it was mid-afternoon. Students shoved and shouted their way out of the high school behind me. As I moved after them, I felt the swirl of bell-bottomed pants around my ankles. The ruffled neckline of my peasant blouse flapped in the wind. I hadn't worn clothes like this since 1975, the year I graduated.

I walked in a haze toward the street. Over the shouts and babble, I heard another noise, shriller, ominous. Daphne McClellan, one of the class misfits, stood in a circle of girls. Her face crinkled in fear. She tried to push through the ring but Jennifer Blake, leader of the popular clique, shoved her back. The girls shrieked as another girl darted in and slapped Daphne's face. A dozen tormenters, their faces distorted with fearsome glee, moved closer to their victim. I could feel the energy shift from teasing to dangerous.

Tears filled Daphne's eyes. She clutched her books to her chest and ducked her head, throwing herself toward a gap in the circle. A fist met her cheek.

Other students were gathering, egging the clique on. I dropped my books and ran toward the mob. "Leave her alone!" I shouted. Jennifer raised her arm to strike again, and I grabbed it, throwing her off balance. She fell against another girl.

"You bitch! Keep your hands off me!" Jennifer growled as she lunged toward me. I dodged, and her momentum carried her past me.

Laughter followed her as she stumbled. Hate filled her eyes as she turned and glared at me. My stomach heaved. Confrontation always made me want to vomit. Why had I gotten involved?

Jennifer started toward me. Instinctively I stuck my hand out like a crossing guard. "Stop!"

She hesitated. I seized the moment. "You want a fight? How about you and me? Or are you scared of one on one?" Even as I prepared for battle, a part of me watched, appalled. I wasn't a fighter and didn't want to be one.

Jennifer glared but didn't rush me. My gaze swept over the others. "Seven against one?" I snorted. "Come on, Daphne." I held out my hand. She slipped through the disjointed circle and ran. I faced the gang, which now looked more hangdog than like curs intent on savaging a lamb.

The sun darkened, and I was back on the Taylors' patio, leaning against Will.

"You okay?" he asked as I straightened.

I brushed a hand over my face. "I think so. I just had the weirdest flashback."

His face was solemn. "I know."

I blinked, wondering if I'd heard him properly.

"Daphne was dyslexic, not retarded," he went on. "What you did that day saved her life. It wasn't the first time those girls had ganged up on her. She was tired. So tired that she was planning on walking into the lake with stones in her pockets, just to end the torment. When you stood up for her, she realized that someone cared."

"But I never spoke to her again," I protested.

Will shrugged. "Once was enough."

The flower's smell gathered strength. I felt his arm encircle me as I fell into a tunnel of night and stars. I came to in a courtroom. A woman sat on the bench, her black robes relieved by a white lace collar. The nameplate in front of her read: "Judge McClellan."

A bailiff handed the judge a folded paper. Daphne read it, then turned to the jury. "Madam Foreperson, what is your verdict in this case?"

A young woman stood. "Guilty, Your Honor."

The defendant, a sullen young man, gave the foreperson a look of loathing. His head snapped toward the judge as she said, "It is the order of this court that you, David Johnson, be remanded to custody until sentencing. And I assure you, Mr. Johnson, that the punishment will fit the crime."

The gavel descended and once more I was back in a winter's night.

"Wow! Daphne a judge." I inhaled deeply and tried to lighten the atmosphere. "Who'da thunk?"

"And you said there was nothing interesting about you." Will shook his head. "Next, you'll be telling me that you just do your job and go home."

I bristled. "Well, I do!"

The now-familiar odor surged up, strong enough to blot out the cold, and I spun into night.

* * * * *

I was sitting on Mr. Clayborne's couch. He lives in the apartment below mine, a few rooms crammed with the detritus of a long life.

Family pictures hung on every wall. Books piled on shelves and floor, fitting companions for the clippings and papers that covered every surface. The air smelled of age and camphor.

The old man tottered into the room, using his cane to steady himself as he carried a cup of tea to me. His hand trembled; a few drops splashed out of the cup onto a rug that hadn't seen a vacuum in weeks.

His voice quavered as he started to speak, and he cleared his throat. "I hate to impose on you, Joan, but I'm so worried. Johnny has filed papers asking that he be appointed my guardian. Says I'm too old to take care of my own affairs." His eyes filled with tears as he handed me the cup and sank down beside me.

I had met my neighbor's grandson, a real piece of work. Smarmy and sly. Not the kind of man you'd want to handle anything. I could tell he was out to get what he could out of Mr. Clayborne—or his estate—and move the old man to a second-rate nursing facility. I wasn't about to let that happen.

"You have some options," I said, sipping the herbal brew. "You can go to court. Or you can tie up your assets so tightly that it will take years for him to cut through the red tape."

Mr. Clayborne looked at me, hope flaring in his eyes. I set the cup down. "I'm not a lawyer," I said, "but I can tell you about some alternatives you have. And none of those include Johnny."

The old man brightened as I outlined his choices. "Joan, you've saved my life!" He patted my knee. "Can you make an appointment with Mr. Sanderson? Soon?"

"Don't worry. I've got you covered." I set down my cup. "I'll even drive you to the office. But you'll have to take a cab home." I walked to the apartment door and stepped through into chill air. I was back at the Taylors'.

Will looked toward the house. "We'd better go back inside. They'll think I've abducted you."

"Wait! What was that last vision about?" I remembered the incident clearly. I'd conferred with my neighbor only a few days before. The meeting hadn't seemed particularly significant, at least not enough to merit a supernatural revisitation.

"Without your knowledge, Mr. Clayborne would have been railroaded by his grandson. With your help, he's now assured of a comfortable old age without having to worry."

He walked toward the French doors. I followed, catching hold of his sleeve as he reached to open them. "Who are you? Charles Dickens? The ghost of Christmas past and present?"

"Just a friend," he answered.

"Some friend! I came for the wine and suddenly I'm in *The Twilight Zone*. And what about Christmas future? Don't you want to show me what's in store for me?"

Will took my face in his hands and looked deeply into my eyes. "I have no power to predict the future. It is yours to tell, the way you want it to be."

"But how?" I asked.

The corsage released its magic once more. No vision this time, just a wavering in the air as I watched Will's face. Images flashed past so quickly I could barely take them in: a house by the ocean; a cabin in the mountains; a spacious home with exquisite furnishings; couples dancing in a posh nightclub; a woman scowling as she worked at her computer; an old lady crying alone; a fresh grave with only one mourner. The last image was of the old man in the flower shop, smiling at me.

The air stilled. Will's face came into focus. "Your choice," he whispered as his finger traced the petals of my flower.

My hand closed over his. As I led him into the house snow began to fall.

MIRACLE IN THE DESERT

Corbett Stiles ducked his head against a biting wind that lifted a lock of black hair from his forehead and pulled his shoulders higher in a useless attempt to keep his ears warm. Patches of snow stretched in the shadows of creosote bushes and ocotillo that spread across the New Mexican desert. Two days before Christmas and Corbett wanted only the humidity and heat of New Orleans instead of the frigid barrenness of this high lonesome place. He wanted beignets and chicory coffee on Christmas morning. Let people who cared about some guy born in a stable guzzle eggnog and hot chocolate. Christmas was for fools and children, and they weren't mutually exclusive.

The two-lane blacktop road stretched to infinity, leaving Corbett reflecting on how he'd come to be in the middle of nowhere. Bidding *adieu* to Bakersfield had been the easy part. A carload of coeds had taken him to Tehachapi. From there, he'd been lucky with rides across California and Nevada, but when a trucker had promised him a ride all the way to Shreveport, he'd fallen for the oldest trick in the book. The driver had assured him that the back roads were just as quick as the interstate and he could avoid the weigh stations that dotted the federal highway. "Don't worry. I done this a thousand times," Ralph had said.

Corbett imagined he had. Had suckered other hitchhikers into desolation, then demanded their packs and wallets at knife point, leaving them to fend for themselves. By the time Corbett could get to the nearest town, Ralph would be half a thousand miles away, and what cop would pursue a complaint brought by a broke, unidentifiable hitchhiker?

Not that he'd had that much in his pack. Just a few clothes, a half-finished bottle of bourbon, and a couple of packs of smokes. The wallet was more of a loss, containing most of his last pay check and his identification. The license could be replaced but he'd never see that four hundred dollars again. His jaw tightened as an urge beat the crap out of Ralph swept over him. Then he sighed. No point in crying over spilt milk—or stupidity.

Dirty yellow light streaked under the flat gray clouds, then disappeared as the sun sank behind a ragged ridge. Corbett pulled his denim jacket collar close around his neck, tucking his chin in to his chest for warmth. The last town they'd passed through was at least seventy miles behind him, so he'd made the decision to walk forward, hoping to find a ranch, a house, a hamlet, before dark. He didn't expect much. "A journey of a thousand miles begins with a single step," he muttered as his boot heels made contact with the asphalt.

Dusk closed around him. The wind died to a whisper. In the distance a coyote chattered. Corbett shivered and walked faster.

A faint hum caught his attention. He stepped onto the shoulder and looked behind him. The drone of an engine grew louder and headlights flickered as a vehicle crept closer. He stuck out his thumb in the classic signal, hoping the driver would not shoot past in a flurry of excess caution. He himself wouldn't stop for a man who had no business being this far away from civilization, especially as night fell. But he had to do something.

A pickup that had been new sometime before the Great Depression slowed as the headlights struck him, and the driver eased toward the shoulder. Corbett held up an arm to shade his eyes from the glare. The driver dimmed the lights. Corbett jogged toward the passenger's door and pulled it open. "Goin' east?" he asked.

"For a bit," the man behind the wheel answered. "Be happy to take you as far as I can."

Corbett hoisted himself onto the seat and slammed the door. "Thanks."

As the driver wrestled the stick shift into first and pulled onto the road, Corbett examined his rescuer in the reflected glow from the headlights. The man looked to be around fifty. He wore a battered cowboy hat and a shearling coat that had seen hard work and heartbreak.

"Where you headed?" the man asked. His voice rasped over the sounds of the rattling truck.

"Nawluns," Corbett drawled, pronouncing it like the native he was.

"Got family there?"

"Used to."

"Going back for Christmas?"

"Christmas is just another day. I maybe got a job on one of the rigs out in the Gulf."

"Oil field, are you?" The man glanced at him.

Corbett nodded. "Sometimes, sometimes not. Been working up by Buttonwillow but the boss got his knickers in a twist because I showed up late a couple of times. So I'm headin' south."

The truck rattled on down the road, the driver silent. A lopsided moon peered through a hole in the clouds, limning the edges with silver, its light turning the high desert a dead blue color. Corbett tried to relax but the memory of the semi driver kept him edgy. He glanced at the man next to him, half expecting him to try something similar, ready if he did. But the man sat at ease behind the wheel, his eyes, and apparently his mind, on the journey.

After half an hour, the truck slowed. The driver glanced at Corbett. "This is where I turn off. Not much out here this time of night. You wanna come into town? Might find a room at the hotel."

Corbett shook his head. "Got no money for a room. Someone will come along sooner or later." He opened the door and started to step out.

The driver looked at him. "Ain't trying to tell you what to do, but you might be out here all night."

The wind nipped Corbett's cheeks. He hesitated, then slid back onto the seat and closed the door. The driver nodded and turned left onto a dirt road that hadn't seen a grader since it had been built. They jolted over a ridge and Corbett saw a handful of lights huddled a couple of miles in the distance. As they pulled into town, he read the sign: Estrella.

The town consisted of a dozen buildings that looked like they'd been built back in the days of the old west. A general store, dark except for a single night light, anchored the row on the right. Next was a hotel, its lobby dimly lit. It butted up against a restaurant and bar. Through the windows Corbett saw people eating and a waitress carrying a tray of food. Across the road a gas station with old-fashioned rolling number pumps crouched in the dim glow of a fixture that shed light on the faded sign. On either side of the station, a couple dozen houses straggled toward the rolling hills covered with yucca and ocotillo. The driver pulled up in front of the hotel and got out. Corbett followed.

They stepped up onto the wooden boardwalk that ran in front of the businesses and Corbett followed the man into the hotel.

"Howdy, Glen," the young woman behind the counter said.

"Evenin', Peggy," the driver replied. "Got me a hitchhiker needs a place to spend the night."

Corbett stepped past the man and nodded to the girl. "Trouble is, I don't have any money to pay you. But maybe . . ." he nodded toward the couch that sat against the wall. "I won't be in your way." He dropped his eyes.

Peggy tossed her blonde hair and smiled. "Just happen to have an empty room. Won't cost you a dime."

"But your boss—"

She cut off Corbett's protest. "I'm the boss." She tossed him a key. "Top of the stairs on the right."

Glen slapped Corbett on the back. "C'mon,

son. Can't sleep on an empty stomach. Stella's still serving supper." He nodded to Peggy and walked out of the hotel. A few strides brought them to the restaurant. Glen pushed the door open and went inside, Corbett on his heels.

Steamy warmth enveloped them as Glen led the way to a corner table and sat down. "I don't know how to thank you—" Corbett began, but Glen cut him off.

"Man needs a little Christmas cheer." He waved to a pudgy woman with long, dark hair who stood behind the bar. "Hey, Stella! Couple of beers."

"Coming right up." She lifted two mugs with one hand and with the other pulled the tap to fill them, then swayed over to their table. "How you doin', Mr. Glen?"

"Just fine, Miss Stella. This here's—" He turned to Corbett. "Never did get your name, son."

Corbett half stood and nodded to Stella. "Corbett, ma'am. Corbett Stiles."

"Nice to meet you, Corbett Stiles." Stella's voice carried the rhythm of Spanish ancestors. She set the beers in front of the men and said, "I got some three-day green chili that's been just waiting for some beef burritos to slide under it."

Glen closed his eyes and grinned. "Bring 'er on." To Corbett he said, "You like hot stuff, Stella's green sauce'll make your tongue do the fandango."

Corbett grinned back. "Sure. Maybe it'll thaw my ears." He looked around the room. A dozen or so men smoked, ate and drank. He wondered how Stella got away with letting them smoke. The state health department would surely raise a fuss if an inspector showed up. He fingered the pack in his shirt pocket, the only thing the trucker had left him, wondering if he had time to light up before dinner but Stella returned, bearing two plates. Corbett sniffed the aroma, spicy and subtle. Melted cheese covered the burritos that swam in a pool of green chilies, pork pieces, and onion. He cut into the meal, glancing at Glen.

The older man sat with his eyes closed and his hands folded, his lips moving as he gave thanks for the food. Corbett dropped his fork and folded his hands in imitation, though he hadn't bothered to speak to God since he'd graduated from St. Dominic's fifteen years ago. He'd shied away from religion and its trappings throughout his travels, depending only on himself as he flitted from job to job, enjoying life on the wild side.

He was used to fending for himself. Dad had skedaddled when Corbett was in high school, leaving Mom to keep their only child fed, clothed, housed, and educated with her salary from her job as a sales clerk at Penney's. As soon as Corbett graduated, he took out, looking for adventure, leaving his mother to her loneliness. She hadn't stayed alone long. When he'd come back a year later, the old house had new tenants and Mom had a new boyfriend who wasn't pleased to find she had a son only a few years younger than he was. So, without regrets, Corbett had hit the road again and hadn't looked back since.

Glen opened his eyes and picked up his fork, a signal for Corbett to eat, too. The first bite went down smooth and tasty. Three seconds later, just as he was raising the second forkful to his mouth, the fire kicked in. His eyes began to water and he coughed. Through the tears he saw Glen smirking as he took another bite, followed by a draught of beer. He grabbed for his beer, letting the brew cool his mouth and throat.

"S'matter, boy? Too hot for you?" Glen handed him the salt shaker. "Salt takes the sear out."

Corbett croaked, "Thanks," shook half a teaspoon into his hand, and licked it clean. The burning eased. As he debated taking another bite, the true taste of the dish caught up with him, leaving him eager for more. He salted the dish heavily and chowed down, suddenly aware of how long it had been since he'd eaten. By the time he'd finished the meal, he considered himself an old hand at Mexican cuisine.

He pushed his plate away and said, "I've had me some Cajun cooking that came close, but nothing like this."

Glen tossed a five-dollar bill on the table and stood up. Corbett stood, too, eyeing the currency. It looked different from any currency he'd seen before, and he wondered how that small amount would cover both dinners and beer. *Guess the locals know best,* he thought as he followed Glen toward the door.

They were almost bowled over by a man who burst into the café, his face contorted with fear. "Sheriff! Donnie's gone missing. Can't find him anywhere!"

Corbett was surprised to find the man speaking to Glen. He had no idea his rescuer was also the local law.

Glen put his hands on the man's shoulders. "Calm down, Wilton. Tell me slow what's goin' on."

Wilton sank into a nearby chair and gasped for breath. "Doris put Donnie to bed near an hour ago. Left the hall light on like always, but when she went to check on him the light was off and he was gone! We've been all over town lookin' for him. We gotta form a search party."

By this time, the entire crowd in the café had risen to circle the distraught man. Glen turned to them and said, "You all ready?" Heads nodded, voices affirmed their willingness to help. Corbett wondered if he was included in the search.

"What's he wearin'?" Glen asked.

"His Lone Ranger pajamas and his church shoes. Didn't take a coat or nothin'. He's gonna freeze out there!"

"Where's Doris?"

"Home now, hopin' he'll show up. He's been so excited about Christmas and Santy Claus comin'. We can't lose him!" His shoulders shook and he put his head in his hands to hide the tears.

Glen lowered his head and clasped his hands once more. Everyone in the place did the same. "Heavenly Father, we got a situation here. You know Donnie and Wilton and Doris. They're good folks and they need your help. Keep Donnie in your care and bring him home safe. Amen"

The final word whispered through the room as Glen raised his head.

One of the women diners started toward the door. "I'll go sit with Doris."

Wilton nodded his thanks and stood up. The prayer had dried his tears and strengthened him. "Tell 'er I'll be home soon—with Donnie."

Glen pointed to different individuals. "Chuck, you and Harley go through every garage, every barn, every place a kid could hide. Wilton and you three, take the south side of town. You two head west, and you two

103

head east. Corbett and I will take the north side. Go slow and don't miss a single place Donnie could've hid."

Stella had come forward, bearing two kerosene lanterns. "There's more in the back. Help yourselves," she said. The searchers headed for the back room.

"Corbett, go grab us a couple." Glen buttoned his jacket, deep in thought.

Corbett followed some other townspeople into Stella's storeroom and came back with two lanterns. He set them both on a table and reached in his pocket for his Bic lighter. Glen's eyes narrowed as Corbett lit their lanterns, but he didn't say anything.

The clouds had moved in again and light snow began to fall. Corbett shivered. It was no night to be out, even dressed for the weather. "Where do you think he might have gone?" he asked Glen.

"Hard tellin'. The boy's only seven and a mongoloid idiot to boot. No sense at all." Glen strode down the street, heading for the end of town opposite of where they'd driven in.

Corbett almost tripped at Glen's description of the missing boy, a description that had disappeared decades ago. He only knew of it because there was a girl who went to St. Dominic's special education classes and he'd heard an old timer speak of her dismissively in those terms. One of the nuns had overheard the man and corrected him. "Down syndrome, please, Mr. Levesque. We don't call people idiots." Glen didn't strike him as a cruel or heartless man, yet the words had fallen so easily from his lips.

He hurried after Glen, who was now passing the last house in town, his right side visible in the light of his lantern, his left only a shadow. By the time Corbett caught up, the road had dwindled to a one-lane track more suitable for a horse than a vehicle.

Glen pointed to the left. "You head up that way. I'll take this side. Now Donnie mightn't take to a stranger, so if you find him, give a yell and I'll come runnin'."

"Gotcha." Corbett held his lantern high and started off into the darkness. He glanced over his shoulder and saw Glen's light bobbing along, getting smaller with every step.

The snow increased, muting the shouts of the other searchers. Corbett filled his lungs and began to call Donnie's name, his voice twisting away on the wind. His head swiveled back and forth as he examined the night for any sign of the missing child. Yucca plants and boulders dotted the land, and his lantern cast eerie shadows as he walked. The ground swelled uphill, and in a few minutes, he was gasping for breath. The elevation and his pack-a-day habit were getting to him.

Snow crept inside his collar. He shivered and shouted again. Cresting a rise, he stopped to scan the land ahead. Setting the lantern on the ground, he shook out a cigarette and ducked his head to light it, cupping his hand around the flame. As he inhaled, he peered into the storm. Flakes eddied, thickening one moment, parting the next. Corbett finished his smoke and tossed the butt into the inch of snow that had already settled. Picking up the lantern, he started down the slope.

Time lost meaning as he searched and shouted through the swirling snow. It was getting harder and harder to see. He traversed the land, hoping for some sign of Donnie or his passage. Finally he gave up. If he got too far from town, he'd never find his way back. Already he was feeling disoriented. Twenty more paces and he'd turn back. He counted them mentally as he moved forward. At the end of the count, he stopped and shouted Donnie's name several times. Nothing but the wind moaning answered him. "God, please let somebody find Donnie," he said as he turned back the way he'd come.

Wait.

A feeling came over him, something he'd never experienced before. Like someone talking inside his mind. He started toward town again.

Turn around.

Corbett looked around and shouted, "Hey! I don't know what you're trying to do, but knock it off."

I will not desert you.

Corbett's thoughts whirled. Who was putting words into his brain? And who wouldn't desert him? His father had. And his mother, along with her new boyfriend, couldn't wait to get rid of him.

Keep looking.

The voice in his head seemed more insistent. Maybe he'd better pay attention.

Feeling like an idiot, he turned and began to walk farther into the snow-whitened desert. "I'll give you a hundred paces," he said to whatever or whomever was intruding with unwanted instructions.

He rounded a boulder and tripped, almost dropping the lantern. He fell to his knees, one hand outstretched to keep him from planting himself face first in the snow. His hand touched cloth. He lifted the lantern higher. The light shone on a small figure curled beside the rock. "Donnie! Donnie! Wake up," he called as he shook the boy.

The child looked up at him, his dark eyes slanted and sleepy. "Aw you Santa's hewper?" he asked.

"No, buddy. I'm helping your dad. You got him panicked, running off like that."

Donnie reached toward him. "I'm gonna find

Santa. He gots toys."

Corbett scooped the boy into his arms, folding his jacket around him to warm him. The boy's feet were bare, his shoes lost somewhere in the night. Corbett hitched him higher and said, "Put your legs around me, okay, buddy?"

Donnie complied, and Corbett tugged the back of his jacket down to cover the icy flesh of the boy's feet. He managed to pick up the lantern and hang it from his elbow as he turned and headed back toward where he hoped Estrella was. In the few minutes he'd spent talking to Donnie, his footprints had vanished.

Snow fell faster and harder, pushed by a strengthening wind. Corbett squinted, trying to see any hint of light through the storm. The wind drowned out any sound but its own low moan. He began to think he was walking in circles. His heart beat faster. Surely God—or whoever had prodded him to go on—wouldn't let him find the lost boy, then abandon them in the storm. He snorted at his foolishness. Hadn't his earthly father abandoned him? Why would God stand by a man who hadn't been in church for years, who barely believed in Him, despite his parochial schooling?

Donnie snuggled closer, shivering, and said, "We goin' home?"

"Sure, kid," Corbett replied. "Just as soon as I figure out where the hell home is."

"My daddy says hell is a bad word. He wash out my mouth when I say it." The boy's voice carried more than a hint of censure.

Chastised, Corbett muttered, "Your dad's right. I won't say it again, okay?"

Donnie smiled. "Okay."

On they went, stumbling into the teeth of the storm. The land fell away in a slight slope. Corbett dug in his heels and sidestepped down the hill until the ground flattened out. A lone cottonwood stood at the bottom of the rise and Corbett sheltered in the lee. He slid down to sit on the icy ground and catch his breath. He set the lantern down and hitched Donnie around, tucking his jacket closer, so he could rub some blood back into the boy's feet.

"I'm cold," Donnie said through chattering teeth.

"Me, too. But we'll be home pretty soon and then you'll warm up quick."

Donnie shook his head. "We lost. We gotta pray. That's what Daddy says." With a solemn upward look, he folded his hands tightly and squinched his eyes shut. "God, help us. We love you. Goodbye." He looked at Corbett. "Now you."

Corbett started to explain his lack of faith, but the confidence on Donnie's face shamed him into closing his eyes and pulling the boy closer as he clasped his hands. "God,

You heard Donnie. We need some help real quick. I know I've never spent much time talking to You, but I hope You'll get us out of this mess. Donnie's mom and dad are waiting. Take us back to them, please. Amen."

He swung Donnie around so the boy could cling to him and hung the lantern over his arm again. He struggled to his feet, trying not to drop the boy. As they stepped out of the shelter of the massive trunk, the wind blew out the lantern, leaving them in darkness. He stood for a moment, trying to orient himself to the way they'd come. Edging forward on his half-frozen feet, he felt the ground begin to rise. Leaning into the slope, Corbett stumbled up the rise, shouting into the night.

At the top of the hill, he stopped and peered around. In the distance a light bobbed. "Here! Over here!" he shouted. He started walking toward the light, and in a few minutes could make out Glen hurrying toward them. Donnie cuddled close as Corbett shouted, "I've found him! He's okay!"

Glen set his lantern down and took the boy from Corbett. "Come here, kid. You scared your ma and pa to death."

Donnie began to wail. "Ma's dead! No!"

"Hey, it's just a figure of speech," Corbett said. "Just a way of saying you scared the crap out of them."

Donnie sniffed. "What's crap?"

Glen glanced at Corbett, then added, "Ask your pa. Your ma's fine. We're gonna get you home to her right now."

Corbett picked up the lanterns and lighted the way as they went back to town.

Two hours later, Corbett trudged up the hotel stairs to his room. He tossed his coat on a chair, sat on the bed and took off his boots, then lay down. He lit a cigarette and watched the snow swirl outside. What if he'd taken the easier downhill walk from the cottonwood? What if he'd been ten feet to the left or right when he was searching for Donnie? What if he'd turned back, ignoring the words in his mind? What if he hadn't taken those few dozen fateful steps that had led him to the boy? What if the trucker hadn't robbed him? What if Glen hadn't come along to give him a lift? If even one of those things had not happened, Donnie would have died in the storm.

It was a long time before he slept.

* * * * *

Christmas Eve day dawned clear and cold. The snow lay unmarked across the land, except in the street, where people had already been up and about. Corbett thanked Peggy for her hospitality and walked over to Stella's to see if she'd give him a cup of coffee before he started the walk back to the highway. Or if Glen was there, maybe he'd give him a lift.

As soon as he walked in the café door, applause broke out. Corbett blushed as Stella hurried over and kissed him on the cheek.

"Breakfast is on me," she said as she hustled him to a table.

"Got some more of that chili?" he asked as he sat down.

"I'll fix you up," Stella promised as she hurried away to get his coffee.

The patrons surged around him, thanks and congratulations in equal measure pouring from their lips. Corbett smiled and nodded and repeated, "I was just lucky," and "Glad I could help." He hadn't had this much adulation in his life. It made him feel real good inside. No longer was he just a rig hand, a rambler, a hell raiser. His existence had made a difference to a boy, a family, and a town.

The door swung open and Glen came in. He headed for Corbett's table and pulled out a chair. "Mind if I set?"

"Sure," Corbett replied.

"Just stopped by Wilton and Doris's place," Glen said as he stirred sugar into the coffee that Stella set before him. "Donnie's doing fine. Didn't get frostbit, for a miracle. It's a damn good thing you found him when you did, though. He wouldn't have lasted much longer in that storm."

"How come he ran off?"

"Said he wanted to go to the North Pole.

Forgot to tell Santa he wanted a toy train when he wrote his letter. Figured if he got to Santa's workshop, he could hitch a ride back in the sleigh."

Corbett shook his head. "Kids, huh?"

"Kids. Gonna be the death of us all, I don't doubt."

Stella set a plate of eggs slathered in green chili in front of him, accompanied by a basket of fresh, warm tortillas. "Glen, you want something?"

He waved her away. "Just coffee, thanks." Then to Corbett, "What're your plans now?"

Corbett shook salt onto his eggs. "Head for New Orleans, I guess. I can still be there by tomorrow if I get good rides."

"You finish up, I'll take you back to the highway."

"I appreciate that." They were quiet as Corbett ate his breakfast and Glen sipped coffee.

Glen signaled Stella for the check as he reached for his wallet. She laughed. "You think I'm gonna charge our hero for his food? Put your wallet away, mister."

The two men nodded their thanks and went out into the sparkling morning. Corbett drew in a breath of pure, cold air and sighed, smiling. They got into Glen's old truck and he swung it in a circle and headed toward the highway. In daylight it seemed a much shorter

113

journey.

The state snowplow had scraped away most of the accumulation of snow, leaving the asphalt steaming in the sun. "Thanks for everything," Corbett said as he opened the passenger's door.

"Thank *you*," Glen responded. He took a bill out of his shirt pocket and handed it to Corbett. "This oughta get you down the road a ways. No, I insist," he said as Corbett tried to give the bill back.

Corbett pocketed the twenty. "Well, might see you all again if I'm ever back this way."

Glen chuckled as if Corbett had said something humorous. "You just get home and enjoy Christmas. We'll do the same."

Corbett climbed down and walked across the highway, waving as Glen spun the truck in a circle and headed back to Estrella. He began walking, keeping an ear open for a possible ride. The sun warmed his face and he began to whistle *Jingle Bells*. He hadn't gotten more than a hundred yards when the sound of tires approaching alerted him. He turned around and stuck out his thumb.

A white Ford F150, spattered with mud, pulled up. Corbett jumped in.

"Where you headed?" the driver, a twenty-something kid, asked.

"South. How far you going?"

"Take you as far as Albuquerque," the kids

114

said, pulling back onto the highway. As they picked up speed, he asked, "What you doing out here in the middle of nowhere?"

Corbett recounted his adventure with the semi driver and how Glen had taken him to Estrella.

The kids scowled at him. "You been smokin' that wacky baccy? Or just drunk?"

Corbett shook his head. "Spent the night there. Went looking for a Down syndrome kid who wandered off into the storm."

"Mister, I don't know where you were last night, but it wasn't in Estrella. That place's been a ghost town for over seventy years. Smallpox went through there in the thirties. Killed almost everybody, and them that survived moved away from the memories. My granddaddy was one who made it through."

"Bull!" Corbett exploded. "I was there. Slept in the hotel. Woman name of Peggy runs it. Had dinner at Stella's place."

The kid hit the brakes hard and swung the truck in a U turn. "Wanna bet?"

"Yeah!" Corbett took the twenty out of his pocket and held it out. "That enough?"

The kid glanced at it. "Don't be tryin' to pass that counterfeit crap off on me!"

Corbett looked closer. The bill was a 1933 silver certificate. He had heard of silver certificates but had never seen one. They'd gone out of circulation by the 1960s.

The kid reached the turnoff to Estrella. As he turned onto the track, Corbett noticed that the snow was unmarked. How was that possible? Glen's truck must have left some reminder of its passing.

In a few minutes they reached Estrella—what was left of it. A couple of stucco walls marked where the filling station had sat. The hotel was only a hole in the ground. Stella's, the houses, the general store had all vanished.

"I don't understand," Corbett whispered. "Where'd it go?"

The kid turned around and headed back to the main road. "Told you, mister. But I'll give you a ride to Albuquerque, anyway. You don't look like a crazy man. And you can keep your phony money." He swung onto the highway and pressed the accelerator. Soon they were flying down the road.

Corbett listened to the kid chatter as the miles spun past, giving grunts or one-syllable responses. As the kid dropped him at the I-40 on ramp, Corbett thanked him. The kid took off in a howl of rubber on pavement.

Corbett stationed himself halfway down the ramp, giving a possible ride ample room to pick him up, and waited. He thought about the heft of Donnie as he held him in his arms, the tang of green chili on his tongue, the good humor of Glen. He thought about prayers and fathers and God. Then he looked skyward. "Thanks for being there," he murmured.

THE TRAIN

Bert Semples sat in the solarium of the Mature Manor rest home, wishing he were somewhere else, anywhere else. Even the early afternoon sunlight couldn't raise his spirits. The day before Christmas always deepened his gloom, if such a thing were possible. All his life he'd been the Grinch, the Scrooge, the doomsayer. Now he was alone and he liked it that way. Except he wasn't really alone. He was surrounded by old folks waiting to die. He probably didn't have long to live, but why did the do-gooders at the county think they had the right to run him out of his own house?

He had been getting along just fine back in Townsend. That little fall didn't amount to a hill of beans, and he didn't need to eat much, just what the wheeling meals folks brought at noon. His house may not have been the tidiest place on earth but he knew where everything was. Here, his sardine can of a room was hardly bigger than his closet back home, but he was always losing things in it. Not that they'd let him bring a lot with him. His little TV, his broken-in recliner (broken down, one of the social workers had said with a sniff), just enough clothes to keep him decent.

"Hi, Mr. Semples. Ready for some lunch?" Rachel, the certified nursing assistant, interrupted his brooding on the wrongs that had been done to him.

Bert scowled. "What slop did the cook mix up today?"

"Homemade potato soup and fresh rolls, the kind you like."

Bert snorted. "Just what the doctor didn't order. Hasn't the cook ever heard of cholesterol?"

Rachel bent close and smiled. "I won't tell if you won't. And I can bring you a tray in here if you want."

Bert nodded and Rachel scampered away. She was the best of the lot who worked here. He wouldn't give two hoots in hell for the doctors and nurses and administrators who were always telling him what he could and couldn't do or eat or have. What the hell did they think they were saving him for? He knew that time was short. Thank God for Rachel, although he would never let her know how he felt. Give people a compliment and they expect one every damned minute. Better to keep them at arm's length. Then they wouldn't pester you to death, wanting money or love from you. He had plenty of the former, none of the latter.

Rachel arrived with his lunch. She set up a small folding table and put his food on it. "There you go, Mr. Semples. Enjoy."

"Hmmph," he muttered as she hurried away. "Haven't enjoyed a damned thing in years. Why should I start now?" Rachel had given him plenty of butter for his rolls, another thing Dr. Hirsh would frown on. He didn't care. His arteries were his own damned business. He buttered a roll and spooned some soup. He had to admit it was pretty damned good.

Rachel appeared as he spooned up the last bite, carrying a piece of carrot cake. She winked, and what could have been a smile turned up the corner of his mouth. She was sure breaking all the damn rules today! What a gal.

When she came back to take the tray away, she said, "There's going to be caroling tonight. Will you join us?"

"Not a chance in hell," he muttered. "Don't believe in all that jollity. Nonsense, if you ask me."

"The kids from the elementary school are coming. They've been practicing for weeks. My Seth can't wait to show off. Sure you won't come down for it?"

"Positive. Now go away and let me be."

As she left, humming a Christmas song, two old women stomped into the sunroom, gossiping and giggling. They were too damn old to giggle, he thought. They started to sit on one of the couches until they spotted him. "Uh-oh," one muttered. "Look who's here."

121

The second one rolled her eyes as Bert glared at her. "Come on, Thelma. Let's go elsewhere." Arm in arm, noses in the air, they stomped out. Bert sighed. He didn't care what two old biddies thought of him. They could go to hell for all he cared.

The room warmed as the sun slanted from the south, and Bert found himself nodding off. Should probably go back to his room and take a nap but he was comfortable here. His head tilted forward until his chin rested on his chest. He began to snore.

He hadn't been asleep long when a hand touched his. He started awake to find a small boy grinning at him. "What the hell do you want?" Bert growled.

The boy, who looked familiar, tugged at his hand. Bert stood up and followed the kid. It wasn't until they were at the front door, not having met anyone, that he realized he'd forgotten his cane. He turned to go back to get it, then realized he was walking just fine. He stretched taller and strode after the boy.

The sun had disappeared in threatening clouds but he didn't feel cold. Neither, apparently, did the boy. He led Bert through streets that seemed at once familiar and strange, finally turning up the walk of a two-story clapboard house with a long porch across the front.

"I know this place!" Bert exclaimed.

The boy grinned and opened the front door, leading the way inside.

Bert stared. There was the familiar fireplace in the living room. His older brother, Randy, stretched to hang an ornament on the tree in the corner. A Christmas carol came from the old radio and his mother hummed along as she strung popcorn and cranberries on a thread.

He grabbed the boy's shoulder. "What have you done? This can't be real. My family's all dead."

The boy nodded toward Bert's mother.

Uneasy, Bert approached the woman. "Mother?" he said.

She glanced up at the boy. "Bertie! I didn't hear you come in. Take off your coat and help Randy finish trimming the tree." She handed the boy the string of popcorn. He went willingly to his task.

Packages had been placed under the spruce. Not many, because the country was still slogging through the Great Depression. Bert bent closer and saw one with his name on it. He reached out and touched it wonderingly. It had been four years since he'd had a gift at Christmas. No, wait. It had been decades since his last Christmas present. His head whirled as time seemed to condense around him.

The front door opened and slammed shut. A

gust of icy wind swirled against Bert's cheeks. A man lurched into the room, his overcoat misbuttoned and his muffler hanging awry.

Bert's mother hustled out of the kitchen. "About time you got home, Clovis," she said, her mouth held tight and thin. "Supper will be ready in a few minutes."

She turned to go back into the kitchen but Bert's father, for that's who had entered, moved forward to block her way. "We can't afford that!" he shouted, pointing to the half-decorated tree.

Mother backed away from his anger. "Mr. Turner down at the grocery gave it to Randy for a dime. It was the last one."

Bert's father stalked over to Randy and grabbed his arm. "Where did you get a dime? Did you steal it?"

Randy, eyes wide and frightened, shouted, "I'm not a thief! I shoveled Mrs. Gramercy's sidewalk and drive. She paid me."

His father's face flushed. "We coulda used that money for something besides a useless tree. Did you ever think of that?"

Randy tried to pull away but Clovis held on tightly.

Mother cried, "Let him alone! The least you can do is let these kids have a bit of holiday."

"And presents! Where the hell did you get

124

money for presents?"

"I saved it!" Mother shouted. "Out of the household money."

Tears washed Bert's eyes. This Christmas was coming back all too clearly. He knew before his father moved what would come next but was helpless to stop what happened.

His father grabbed the first present he could reach, which happened to be the one with Bert's name on it.

Both Berts cried, "No! Not that one! That's from Santa!"

Clovis ripped the paper off and tore open the box, revealing a red locomotive with a blue coal car attached. "How dare you!" he shouted at his wife.

Bertie wept as he cowered behind his brother. "Don't, Daddy! Please don't!" he cried.

Turning to his younger son, Clovis ripped the coal car loose and smashed it to the floor. The red engine bounced off the wall. Wheels flew in all directions and the smokestack rolled across the room to rest under the armchair.

Bertie sobbed. "I asked Santa for that!"

Clovis grinned lopsidedly. "You dumb kid. There's no such person as Santa Claus. Never was, never will be." With that he turned and staggered toward the kitchen.

The scene spun before Bert's eyes and he

felt himself falling.

He came to in his chair in the sunroom. The sun had dropped behind the line of pines, sending shadows across the snow. Bert shivered. Slowly he rose, leaning on his cane, and made his way to his room. He lay down on the bed and fell asleep.

Soft whistling woke him. A young man sat in the chair reserved for guests. Until now, only staff had used it. Bert never had visitors. The young man smiled. A hint of sadness stained his gaze. Without speaking he held out his hand.

Bert swung his legs over the side of the bed and stood up, barely noticing that the constant ache in his hips had gone away. With a sense of inevitability, he followed the young man out of the room, down the hall, and out into the remnants of evening. The thermometer outside the main entrance read well below freezing but Bert felt no chill as he and the young man strode quickly along the sidewalk.

In only a few minutes they came to a nightclub. At least that's what they used to be called, Bert mused. Now they were bars, full of televisions tuned to a thousand different channels, the sound turned off or turned to earsplitting. Instead of elegant dinners they served pub grub, whatever the hell that was.

Warm air breathed over them as they went inside. A ball of mistletoe hung in the arched doorway that led from the foyer into the main room. Small tables decorated with sprigs of holly and red candles were grouped intimately around a stage where a trio played old jazz standards. Along the far wall stretched a mahogany bar backed by a mirror that reflected bottles and glasses. Several patrons sat on stools, chatting with the bartender or their companions.

Bert noticed one woman in particular. Her blonde hair was pulled up in a French twist, with a few loose strands curling around her face. She leaned in, smiling, to the man sitting next to her. Bert recognized him. Frank Dunlap, his best friend from college. The girl leaned closer and Frank kissed her lingeringly. Then, as though looking for someone, she turned toward the door.

Bert's heart jumped so that he was afraid he was having a coronary. Stella Untermach's eyes swept past as if she didn't see him. They landed on the young man with him as he walked toward her, his eyes glistening with hurt and tears.

From his distance Bert couldn't hear their words but they had been etched on his heart sixty years earlier. He wiped angrily at the tears that echoed the young man's tears. He wanted to leave, to not relive his breakup with the only woman he had ever loved, but he was held fast, as if a spell had been cast.

The young man wheeled away from the couple. Stella reached to stop him but he had already rejoined Bert. Without speaking they returned to the home. No one was in the halls as the young man led Bert back to his room. And then the young man faded away.

Bert sat on the edge of his bed, still stunned by the memory of Stella and Frank. He thought he'd gotten over that hurt long ago. Now he realized that he'd just covered it over with scars, scars that the young man had torn open.

Rachel appeared in the doorway and flipped on the light. "Hi, Mr. Semples. Ready for dinner?"

Bert shook his head. "Not tonight."

Rachel said, "It's baked chicken and rice."

He lay back on the bed. "Leave me alone."

Rachel left, quietly closing the door, leaving him to his memories.

Drowsiness overcame Bert but he struggled against it. He didn't want any more adventures into the past. He didn't want to shed any more tears. He wanted to shut his heart up again, hold firm against the pain of betrayals he'd experienced all his life.

A glow in the corner of the room caught his attention. A figure stood there, wrapped in light so soft that he could barely make out her features. He only knew that it was a woman, perhaps by the way she stood. The glow brightened. She glided closer. Reaching out, she laid a glowing hand on his chest just above his heart.

Bert tried to move but found himself paralyzed. Was he dying?

Her laugh was like the sound of tiny Christmas bells. "You are alive and likely to remain so," she said.

"What are you doing to me?" Bert croaked. He cleared his throat. Surely a dying man wouldn't have to clear his throat.

"Watch." At the whispered word, a movie screen seemed to roll out on the ceiling of his room. A man in a business suit and tie sat at a ruthlessly tidy desk, perusing some papers. Bert recognized his forty-year-old self. A knock at the door interrupted him. "Come in," he barked.

Leslie Darden, his secretary, came in and set a sheaf of papers on his desk. "Mr. Moyer dropped these by for your signature."

Bert remembered the incident. As he watched the scene unfold, he felt himself blushing. In the movie, he snapped, "Doesn't he think I have anything better to do than his paperwork? I spend my time on really important clients, the ones with enough money to make my efforts worthwhile." As he scowled and focused on scanning and signing the papers, he failed to see Leslie's expression.

Her sweet face shone with love. Her pink lips smiled and her lovely brown eyes looked at him adoringly.

Bert's eyes filled as he watched his movie alter ego tap the papers into alignment and shove them back at her without looking up. Her face crumpled and her shoulders slumped as she left the office.

He had never realized that she was in love with him because he'd been too wrapped up in making and keeping money and nursing a grudge against Stella and Frank.

Before he could sniff back his tears, another movie began on the ceiling. The angel's hand stayed at his heart.

On the ceiling, Bert walked through the large room where the draftsmen worked. He employed fifteen men and resented every paycheck he signed. Money that went to them was money that went away from him. He had stewed and fretted over this for months and finally decided to cut the hours of the three newest men. As he passed Joel Steen's drafting table, Steen, the last man hired, spoke up.

"Mr. Semples, could I talk to you for a moment?"

Bert frowned. "What is it, Steen?"

The man lowered his eyes. "It's about the cut in hours, sir. I really can't afford to lose five hours a week." His face flushed.

Bert said briskly, "Sorry, Steen. Business has fallen off. I can't justify paying you for full time."

"But, sir," Steen protested, "We're all working as hard as we can and we still can't keep up. I don't understand why hours have to be cut. We don't have enough time to do our work now."

Bert's lips thinned. "Are you quite finished, Mr. Steen?"

The man hung his head.

"Plan ahead, that's my motto. Men like you should have money put away for times like these." He walked on, barely acknowledging the hellos of the others.

For a moment he felt a twinge. Business wasn't that bad, and he knew there was enough work to keep them all busy, but every nickel he could squeeze out of his payroll was cash he could count on in his old age. And losing five hours a week certainly shouldn't break any man who had the foresight to plan for the future.

The movie switched to a dark street. Steen walked along, head down. Christmas lights blinked from trees set in apartment windows. The faint sounds of a carol rose through the night air. Steen walked up a set of stairs and took out a key, letting himself into the apartment building. He trudged up to the second floor and went into a small apartment. As he hung his coat and hat in a hall closet, the sound of a woman's voice came to him.

"Honey, is that you?"

Steen pasted a smile on his face. "Who else but your one and only?" He walked into a small living room where a woman lay on the couch, a knitted throw over her legs. Her face was pale and dark shadows circled her eyes.

Steen leaned over to kiss her.

She touched his cheek and smiled, a winsome smile touched with sadness. "How was your day? Did you talk to Mr. Semples about your hours?"

Steen turned away from her hopeful look. "He said he couldn't afford to put me back to full time. I'm sorry, Helen."

A small girl of about five ran into the room. "Daddy! Daddy! You're home!"

Steen swept her up in a bear hug and nuzzled into her neck, causing her to giggle. "My darlin' Cindy. Were you Momma's helper today?"

The girl nodded vigorously. "I helped her fix lunch and rubbed her arms when they hurt. She said I'm her bestest helper."

"You sure are," he said as he set her down. "We couldn't get along without you."

Cindy ran over to the small Christmas tree that sat in a corner of the room. She touched the ornaments one by one. "I love Christmas," she said. "Do you think Santa got my letter?'

"Santa gets every single letter," her mother assured her. "Only sometimes his elves are so busy they can't keep up with the toy demands."

"Oh, they'll find time to make my Betsy Wetsy doll," Cindy said, nodding sagely. "That's all I want Santa to bring." Humming a Christmas tune, she skipped off to her room, intent on some mysterious errand that only a five-year-old could accomplish.

Steen and his wife exchanged looks. Their daughter wanted only the most expensive doll on the market, and there was no way to buy it for her. They had barely been able to pay Helen's medical bills, and since Steen's hours had been cut at the beginning of November, they were falling behind on the grocery bills and the rent. There was no way to get their daughter her deepest desire.

Steen knelt beside his wife and took her in his arms. "I love you so much."

"And I you."

Together they wept.

The scene faded. More tears gathered in Bert's eyes and ran down his wrinkled cheeks.

The angel spoke. "These are the gifts you could have had and turned away from. The gift of love and the gift of charity."

"Did Steen's wife get better?" he asked.

"Don't you remember?" the angel replied.

Bert thought hard. Steen had left the company not long after the new year. He sort of remembered Leslie taking up a collection for something around that time, but he was too busy—or too cheap—to contribute. Something about flowers or a funeral wreath.

The angel took her hand away from his heart.

Bert scooted up in bed. "But I didn't know! If I had I would have ..." his voice drained away. What would he have done? Probably nothing. He'd been too self-involved all his life. He had never had empathy or sympathy for anyone. He had been too busy wallowing in his own misery.

The angel stepped away from the bed. Her glow faded.

"Wait!" Bert called. "How can I make it up?"

"You can't," she said softly. "You can never go back and do things again. You can only go forward. As you do, remember that you must give to receive. And you have only this moment that you can be sure of. The rest is a mystery." Then she was gone.

Bert sat up, reaching for the last remnants of her glow as it faded away. He swiped at the dampness on his grizzled cheeks. If only he had known then. He would have saved Steen's wife. Or at least made sure they didn't have to worry about her medical bills. He would have smiled at Leslie and actually seen the love she had for him. He would have loved her back. She was a wonderful woman, he now realized. Only he'd been too sour and busy to see that. And now he had only this moment.

From down the hall he heard voices, a lot of voices. Young voices, old voices. The children must have arrived to sing to the residents.

He limped to the closet and got out his fancy Christmas tie that his brother had sent him, to soften his guilt for not visiting, Bert had assumed. Now he saw it as a gift instead of a payoff. He slid it under his collar and buttoned the top button of his shirt. Working slowly because of his arthritic fingers, he knotted the tie. Then he slipped into the one sport coat he'd brought. Going to the mirror over the sink, he combed his hair. Then he brushed his teeth to get rid of the scum that his naps had left. For surely they must have been dreams, not real events. He couldn't have met himself at different ages. It just wasn't possible.

When he was presentable, he took his cane and walked down the hall as briskly as he could. The common room was crowded with residents watching a line of children about eight years old. The children sang lustily if not harmoniously. Two children shook jingle bells in time to the song.

He found a vacant chair and sank into it. His foot began to tap in time to the music. One of the little boys caught his eye and smiled as he sang. Bert's heart lifted.

The concert ended and the children scattered to their parents. The little boy who had smiled at Bert ran to Rachel and flung his arms around her. "Did I sing good, Mama?" he said.

Rachel hugged him. "The best. You'll be on *America's Got Talent* before you know it," she said. Then she led the boy over to where Bert sat.

"Mr. Semples, this is my son, Seth. Say hello to Mr. Semples, son."

The boy stepped forward and held out his hand. "Hello, sir."

Bert shook the tiny hand, impressed by the boy's manners. "Pleased to meet you, Seth."

"Do you have a little boy?" Seth asked.

"No, I don't, I'm sorry to say." Bert wondered briefly what his children and Leslie's would have been like if he only hadn't been too stubborn to pay attention.

"That's too bad," Seth said.

"Okay, son, let's go get some cookies and egg nog and leave Mr. Semples in peace," Rachel said.

Bert stood up. "May I have a moment, Rachel?"

She looked at him inquiringly.

Bert coughed. "Just want to thank you for taking care of us old farts. For taking care of—for caring about me."

Rachel blushed. "Just doing my job," she said, attempting levity.

He gazed deep into her eyes. "You're doing much more than that, and you know it." He touched Seth's shoulder. "Now then, I think I'd like a cookie or two. You suppose you could show me where they are?"

Seth took his hand. "Sure."

As they walked toward the table at the back of the room where the refreshments were piled high, Bert felt the warmth and joy of the child beside him seep into his burdened heart.

"After we get cookies, we get presents," Seth chattered. "Mom said." He pointed to the Christmas tree in one corner of the room. Presents had been piled around it while Bert was having his date with the angel. He remembered that there had been a donation box in the dining room since Thanksgiving, asking residents to contribute toward presents for the children. Bert had ignored the plea. Now he regretted that choice.

After eating a frosted Santa cookie trimmed with silver sprinkles and sipping a paper cup of egg nog, he and Seth went to the corner where the tree stood. Bert sat in a chair and Seth sat at his feet.

"What do you want Santa to bring you?" Seth asked.

"Boy, I'm too old for Santa to care about."

"Nobody's ever too old," Seth said firmly.

As the head administrator picked up packages and called out names, Bert was surprised to realize that there were also presents for the residents. The staff must have chipped in, or there must have been some provision made from the outrageous residence fees they charged to give each one something.

Seth got his present but didn't open it.

"Don't you want to see what Santa brought?" Bert prodded.

"I'm waiting for you to get yours so we can open them together."

Bert chuckled. "I doubt that I'm going to get anything. I haven't been a good boy like you."

Just then the administrator called his name and, smiling, handed him a present. Bert blinked. Where had that come from? Certainly not Santa.

Seth wiggled. "Now we can open them!"

Together they tore into the bright paper packages. Seth jumped up and did a little dance when he saw his miniature Lego set.

Bert was too stunned to move. In his hands he held a red locomotive attached to a blue coal car, just like the one his father had broken so many years before.

Harry, one of the oldest residents, wandered past, stopping to look at the train. "Boy, you got a peach there," he said. "I used to collect antique toys. Had one of those. Company quit making them in 1940 or thereabouts. Wonder where that one came from? Somebody sure likes you to part with something like that." He moved on to say hello to a couple of children.

Stunned, Bert watched him walk away. Where *had* the toy come from?

Seth leaned against Bert's knee, reaching out to touch the train. "Santa really likes us, sir."

Bert held the train to his heart. "He sure does, boy. He sure does."

THE AUDIT

"Good night, Mr. Trumbull. Have a merry Christmas."

"Same to you, Ms. Green." Gordon Trumbull buttoned his topcoat with one hand, his other occupied with an overloaded briefcase. Without looking at the receptionist for the Department of Child Welfare, he pushed through the revolving door into blue twilight. A late December crescent moon on its way to the horizon tangled in the bare branches of an elm tree. Last week's snow lingered in drifts against the buildings and in heaps against the curbs, piled up by plows.

Gordon hurried to his car, eager to get home to the peace and quiet of the long holiday weekend. Christmas was, in his opinion, the most untidy and unbalanced holiday of them all. Shoppers shoved and stomped through Black Friday midnight openings, grabbing bargains with the fervor of '60s radicals. Trash bins would soon overflow with wrappings, boxes, and leftover food. Money flew about like starlings, scattered hither and yon, all in the name of love. As if presents could buy anyone's love. He had first-hand experience of how false that premise was. One ex-wife and several former lovers had taught him not to offer his devotion as freely as he'd done when he was younger. He preferred to live as he worked, in neat columns that balanced at the end of the day and left no room for errors, either of mathematics or of the heart.

As one of the county auditors, he roamed from the DMV to Health and Human Services to the planning section and further, checking each department for bookkeeping errors. He hadn't missed the eye rolls and head shakes that the other employees thought were surreptitious as he passed among them. He didn't really care. His job was to keep the county solvent and deter budding embezzlers. All the mess of interpersonal relationships, gossip, and holiday cheer left him cold.

His headlights mingled with a thousand other Friday night commuters as he drove home. Strip malls, discount stores, and Christmas tree lots were packed with last-minute shoppers. He relaxed into the seat, smirking at those frenzied bargain hunters plunging into penury for the next six months as they bought their offspring, their relatives, and themselves gifts that would be passé by the end of the year. For ninety percent of the population, regrets outstripped resolutions by the time February rolled around. Fortunately he was in the other ten percent.

The neighborhood sparkled with lights as

he turned onto his street. Plastic Santas waved from front yards. Twinkling reindeer hauled sleighs across roofs. Inflatable giant snowmen billowed with compressed air. Gordon shook his head at the electrical excess as he pulled into his drive, pushing the garage door remote. His was the only house on the block without so much as a wreath at the entry. The garage door slid shut behind him, and he went into the kitchen through the connecting door. He laid his briefcase on the breakfast bar that separated the kitchen from the living room and shrugged out of his coat. As he walked toward the bedroom, he loosened his tie. It was good to be home.

After he'd changed into khakis and a polo shirt, Gordon flipped on the television and mixed up some Hamburger Helper. He opened a bottle of mineral water and sat on the couch while his dinner cooked. The usual Christmas lineup of syrupy movies occupied almost every channel. Even ESPN had resorted to reruns of game highlights. He pushed the off button, tossed the remote on the coffee table, and went to stir the pot. The phone rang.

"Hello." He cradled the receiver between ear and shoulder as he opened another bottle of water.

"Mr. Trumbull, this is Hope Bascomb from Child Protection. Two brothers have just come in. They need a place to stay tonight and possibly tomorrow night, too. All our foster homes are full. Can you help us out?"

"Ms. Bascomb,. I'm not certified for foster care—"

"Please, Mr. Trumbull." Her voice rose, and he heard the quaver. "Their mother's in the detox unit, coming down off meth. There *is* nowhere else to put them, except juvenile hall, and they're preschoolers, not criminals."

Gordon ran a hand over his face. "How old?"

"Five and three. They're nice boys, just frightened and confused right now."

"All right. Bring them on over."

Hope sighed. "Thank you, Mr. Trumbull. We'll be there within twenty minutes. You won't regret this."

Wanna bet? Gordon thought as he hung up. He went into the guest room and turned down the bed, then put out clean towels in the bathroom. The only children he'd been close to had been his brother's children, but they were in high school and college now. Years had passed since he'd had to baby-sit toddlers. He wondered how he'd amuse them for two days.

The doorbell rang. Ms. Bascomb and the boys had arrived.

Hope held the smaller boy in her arms; the older one huddled close to her side, gripping her hand as if he never wanted to let go. "Mr.

144

Trumbull, meet Kevin and Kyle Horner," Hope said.

Gordon stepped aside and ushered Hope and the kids in. "Hello, boys," he said. "Which one are you?" he asked the older as he closed the door.

The boy hung his head; dark hair fell over his brow. "Kevin," he murmured.

Hope set the smaller boy down. "Boys, Mr. Trumbull will be taking care of you for the weekend." Her bright hair glowed against her hunter green coat. Her dark eyes sparkled and her lips were full and pink. She looked as if Christmas had been made just for her, as if the joy of the season flowed from her heart. Gordon had a hard time imagining her dealing with the horrors that confronted child welfare workers on a daily basis.

Hope started to take Kevin's coat off, but the boy clutched the frayed woolen jacket. She knelt and looked into his dark eyes. "It's okay. Mr. Trumbull will keep it safe."

Kevin shook his head.

Gordon said, "Let him keep it on if it makes him feel better. What about pajamas? And clothes for tomorrow?" he asked.

"What you see is what you get." Hope's voice was flippant but her eyes held pain. "I have to run. Other business to take care of." She stooped to give each boy a hug and a kiss. "Be good boys and I'll see you soon." Then she was gone in a gust of snow-scented air.

Gordon looked at the kids standing lost and lonely. "Are you hungry?" he asked.

"You got supper?" Kyle's voice was soft and sweet. His blue eyes gazed at Gordon with pure innocence.

"You like Hamburger Helper?"

Kyle nodded vigorously. Kevin sniffed the air, his eyes darting everywhere.

Gordon turned toward the kitchen. "Dinner's just about ready. You want some milk?"

Kyle scampered after him, but Kevin lingered in the living room, still clutching his jacket around him. Gordon pulled out a chair and Kyle clambered onto it, kneeling and leaning his elbows on the table, his expression eager.

"Come on, Kevin." Gordon pulled out another chair. The older boy sidled into the room as if scouting for hidden danger. He slipped onto his chair and folded his hands on the table, which hit him just below the chin.

Gordon noticed that their hands were grubby but decided that cleanliness could wait. He poured two glasses of milk and set them in front of the boys. By the time he'd dished the dinner onto plates, their glasses were empty and their mouths rimmed with milk.

"You boys must be hungry," Gordon said as he set the plates of food on the table.

146

Kevin reached for his fork. "We din't have no lunch."

"Or brekkus," Kyle chimed in around a mouthful of macaroni and hamburger.

Gordon watched, astonished at how quickly the food disappeared. His nieces and nephews had never put away their dinners the way these kids did.

Kevin finished first and cast a longing glance toward the pot on the stove. Gordon sighed and spooned more food onto the plates. At this rate, the two would empty the pantry by morning. As the boys finished what was to have been his dinner, Gordon rummaged in the fridge for cheese and bologna, which he slapped between slices of bread. He sat down and munched as the boys cleaned their plates for the second time. At last the two seemed to be filled, and Kevin relaxed enough to take his coat off.

"How about a bath?" Gordon asked after he'd loaded the dirty plates and glasses in the dishwasher.

Kevin gave him a sidelong glance. "Together?"

"Well, you and Kyle together," Gordon said. "I'll shower in the morning."

"Okay." Kevin slid from his chair and took Kyle's hand as Gordon led the way to the bathroom.

Gordon ran water into the tub. "This too

hot?" he asked. Kevin touched the stream gingerly, then shook his head. "It's okay. You can go now." His eyes held suspicion and a touch of fear.

"No problem. Call me if you need me." Gordon backed out of the room, leaving the door slightly ajar, as Kevin began to help Kyle disrobe.

"Can I come in and get your clothes?" he called.

"I guess," Kevin replied. "But no peeking."

"No peeking," Gordon agreed. He gathered up the boys' jeans and shirts and other things, keeping his head averted. As the boys played in the tub, he tossed their clothes in the washing machine. By the time he got back to the bathroom with a couple of his tee shirts in lieu of pajamas, the two had turned the floor into a slippery mess. Gordon clenched his teeth and didn't yell at them.

"Need some help drying off?" he asked, holding up a towel. "I promise, no peeking."

Kevin stepped out of the tub and Gordon wrapped the towel around him, patting his back, chest and arms dry. "I guess you can do your legs," he said. He turned his back as Kevin finished drying himself, then handed him a shirt. "Best I can do on short notice."

By the time he'd mopped up the bathroom floor and tucked the boys into the double bed in the guest room, Gordon was ready for bed, too. He'd never realized how much energy children brought into a house.

Kyle's eyes were at half mast but Kevin watched Gordon with wary eyes. "Kyle's scared of the dark," he said, his voice quavering.

"I'll leave the hall light on," Gordon promised. He turned off the overhead light and flipped the hallway switch. Kevin's eyes glinted.

Gordon sighed. "Want me to tell you a story?"

Kevin nodded.

Gordon settled on to the edge of the bed and tucked the spread around Kevin's chin. "Once upon a time . . ."

* * * * *

On Saturday, Gordon woke to the sound of the television. He stumbled down the hall in his pajamas and found the boys sitting cross-legged in front of the set, watching a cartoon that involved explosions, howls, and spinning stars. He grabbed the remote and dialed the sound down six notches.

He started a pot of coffee brewing and took the boys' clothes out of the dryer. By the time the coffee was ready, the boys were dressed.

Kyle tagged along into the kitchen and climbed onto his chair as Gordon went in to pour himself a cup of coffee. "I really,

really like Cap'n Crunch," he said as Kevin slipped into his seat.

"That a cartoon?" Gordon looked over the cup rim at the boy.

Kevin and Kyle snickered. "It's cereal!" Kevin said, pouncing on Gordon's mistake.

"Sorry. I don't have any of that. How about some bran flakes?" Two head shook in unison. "Scrambled eggs?"

The boys looked at each other. "We din't ever have them," Kevin said. Their gazes held Gordon immobile. How could kids get to be this age without ever having had a scrambled egg?

He took out the fixings for scrambled eggs, toast, and hot chocolate. As he stirred and mixed, the boys kept up a running commentary on his house. Where did he keep his clothes? How come the floor was empty? Why didn't he let them sleep on the sofa like they did at home? Did he have a car? Did he have some toys?

The boys tasted the eggs gingerly, then ate like trenchermen. By the time Kyle had finished his third piece of toast and jam, Gordon began to wonder where it all was going.

After breakfast, he loaded the boys into the car and headed for the nearest discount store. He hoped he wouldn't get busted for not having them in secured booster seats.

Kyle sat in the shopping cart, his tiny hands patting Gordon's as they pushed through the crowd. Kevin wanted to walk, but Gordon deposited him in the basket. "What would Ms. Hope say if I lost you?" he asked.

"She'd be real mad," Kevin said solemnly. "She would get you in trouble."

"Right. So that's why you have to ride."

He bought each boy a toothbrush, a comb, mittens, caps, underwear, pajamas, shirts, and jeans. As they passed the shoe department, he glanced at Kyle's ratty tennis shoes. Within minutes, each boy had a new pair of fleece-lined boots.

A stop in the grocery department netted a box of Cap'n Crunch and food for the next couple of days. Gordon might as well feed the boys well while they were with him.

On the way to the checkout, they passed the toy department. Kyle's eyes were riveted on the bounty, and Kevin held on to the cart, resting his chin on his hands as he watched the toys pass. But neither one said a word.

As they pulled into the drive, the wind rattled the branches of the oak in Gordon's front yard. The sky darkened and the horizons smudged. "Looks like there's a storm on the way," Gordon said as he ushered the boys into the house.

They whiled away the afternoon with videos and a deck of Go Fish cards left from long ago. Gordon taught them to play, then left them to it while he sautéed pork chops, baked a couple of potatoes, and made a salad. At dinner, Gordon was once again astounded at how little the boys seemed to know about regular life. And anger rose in him, anger against the druggie mom and God knows what scumbags she'd exposed the boys to in their short lives. They were *good* boys, and they deserved better than to be treated like unwanted garbage.

After they'd "helped" him put the dishes in the dishwasher and clean up the kitchen, Gordon said, "Would you like to take a walk and look at the Christmas lights? Try out your new boots?" The moment the words were out of his mouth, he regretted them. But the boys looked so eager, he couldn't back out.

Within minutes, they walked out into the night, bundled up like Arctic explorers. The wind had died, but snow fell gently, large and soft as winter butterflies.

Kyle and Kevin held onto his hands, scuffing through the snow and giggling. Each lighted house dazzled them. They pointed and oohed, faces shining. Gordon began to see the night through their eyes. He thought of his childhood: helping his father and mother decorate the tree, stringing lights through the bushes outside, the excitement of wrapping presents behind closed doors, the agony of waiting until Christmas morning to find out what Santa had left. He wondered if Kevin and Kyle had ever had a real Christmas.

They walked down one side of the street and crossed over, then walked back toward Gordon's house. As they neared the corner, Kyle's steps slowed and he reached up. Gordon scooped him up. Kyle's head sagged against Gordon's shoulder and a mittened thumb went to his mouth.

Kevin scampered to the next display. It was a simple nativity scene. Wooden sheep, cows, and donkeys stood aside for a shepherd and three magi in painted robes. All gathered around the simple stable wherein Mary and Joseph kept watch over the Christ child.

"Who's that?" Kevin pointed at the cradle.

"That's the baby Jesus," Gordon replied. "He's the reason we have Christmas."

Kevin looked puzzled. "Not Santa?"

Gordon chuckled. "Nope. Jesus was God's only begotten son. He was born in a stable in Bethlehem. The wise men and shepherds followed a big, bright star to the stable. The wise men, those tall guys, brought him gifts of gold, frankincense and myrrh."

"That's funny presents. Why din't they bring him a fire engine or some little cars?"

"They didn't have fire engines and cars back then. And the presents were to show how precious Jesus was. God sent him to Earth to teach us how to love one another."

"He doesn't love us. Mom said nobody loves us 'cept her. Dave said he loved me, but Mom made him go away 'cause she said that was creepy."

Gordon bit back a curse. He was getting the Cliff's Notes course on child abuse. He didn't want to read the whole book. "Come on, Kevin. It's getting late. Time for bed."

Kevin took Gordon's free hand as they sauntered toward home amid eddying flakes. "How come you don't got a Christmas tree?" the boy asked.

Gordon pondered the question. How to tell a little boy just finding out the real meaning of Christmas that he didn't believe in all the hype and hoorah? Finally he said, "Because I didn't know you and Kyle would be coming to spend Christmas with me. When it's just one person, it seems a little silly to put up decorations and then take them down again."

Kevin slipped in the snow and Gordon pulled him upright. They reached the house, but Kevin stopped and surveyed the austere façade. "When I'm a big man, I'm going to have a Christmas tree even if it's just me and Kyle. And I'll invite Jesus to come and look at it. And I'll give him presents, just like them guys."

The porch light reflected on the falling snow, and for a moment, Kevin's head seemed surrounded by a milky halo. A wandering wind tossed the flakes heavenward, and the illusion vanished.

After the boys, teeth brushed and new pajamas on, were tucked into bed, Gordon called the teen girl who lived just down the street. "Tiffany, can you come watch a couple of boys for about half an hour?"

"Mr. Trumbull, it's Christmas Eve!"

"Twenty bucks in it for you."

"I'll be right over."

Gordon hung up the phone and within five minutes, Tiffany stood in the living room.

"The boys are asleep and shouldn't be a problem," Gordon said as he handed her cash. "I'll be back as soon as I can."

Traffic was sparse and the parking lot mostly empty as Gordon arrived at the discount store. He hurried inside and picked up a small, pre-lighted Christmas tree and some wrapping paper, already discounted by fifty percent. A couple of stockings, some candy, a set of miniature cars and a fire truck, complete with tiny firemen and hydrants, went into the basket.

After he'd sent the sitter home, he cleared a space on the coffee table and plugged in the tree. The colored lights blinked and winked. He filled each stocking with some candy, then wrapped the toys in bright red and green paper. Kyle's name went on the fire engine and Kevin's on the cars. He tiptoed into the guest room and laid the stockings at the foot of the bed. Then he unplugged the tree and went to bed.

He woke before dawn, eager to be up before the boys. He plugged in the tree, letting the lights illuminate the room. He made coffee and sat in the dimness, remembering. And wondering about Kyle and Kevin and what they would return to.

Whispers from the bedroom drew him in. The boys knelt on the bed, staring at the stockings.

"Merry Christmas," Gordon said.

"These ours?" Kevin touched the fake fur trim on the one closest to him.

"I don't see any other little boys in here, so they must be."

"Santa came!" Kyle squealed, clutching his stocking to his chest.

"Come on. I'll fix some breakfast." Gordon shooed the boys, still holding their stockings, ahead of him so they wouldn't see his grin.

The boys entered the living room and stopped as if they'd run into a wall. Tree lights sprinkled radiance over the packages beneath it. Gordon put a hand on each boy's back and nudged them forward.

The two touched the gifts as if they expected them to vanish. "Hey! This one's mine!" Kevin reached for it, and Gordon put Kyle's into his little hands.

"Looks like Santa found you," he said.

"Or the wise men," Kevin said, laying his stocking on the table and tearing at the paper-wrapped box.

"Maybe Jesus!" Kyle exclaimed as he dropped his stocking and fumbled at his present with tiny fingers.

Within minutes the boys were playing happily with their toys, sharing and singing their version of *Rudolph the Red-Nosed Reindeer.*

Gordon sat on the couch, basking in their joy, wondering how he could have spent so many years playing Scrooge. For less than the cost of a pair of movie tickets he'd brought bliss to a couple of children that most people seemed to have forgotten. And it hadn't hurt a bit.

The doorbell rang. Gordon jumped up to answer it. Hope Bascomb stood outside.

"Ms. Bascomb! Come in. We're just celebrating Santa's visit."

As she stepped inside, Hope brought a scent of pine and snow. Her face glowed, reminding Gordon even more of an angel. "Hey, guys," she said.

"Look! Look what Santa brought!" The boys surged toward her, holding up their gifts and beaming like their lives were perfect.

After Hope had exclaimed over their treasures, she said, "Why don't you boys get dressed? We have to go soon."

As the two scampered off, she said to Gordon, "We found an aunt who's willing to take them in until their mother is feeling better."

Gordon was surprised to feel his heart drop. "Can't you leave them just for today?"

Hope shook her head. "The aunt's only in town for a couple of hours. I really have to get them to her or they'll end up in foster care."

Gordon nodded, swallowing back a lump in his throat. "We'll be right out."

* * * * *

On Monday morning, Gordon got to the office early. At eight o'clock, he dialed the number for Child Welfare. "Ms. Green, I'd like to speak to Hope Bascomb."

"I don't have her in our employee directory," Ms. Green replied after a moment's search.

"Of course she works there. She brought me a couple of children to care for over Christmas."

"I'll put you through to Mr. Lancaster. He's in charge of foster care."

After a couple of clicks and a moment of Muzak, Lancaster came on the line. Gordon explained what had transpired over the weekend.

"I'm sorry, Mr. Trumbull. We had no children without foster care this weekend. We made sure of that," Mr. Lancaster said.

Gordon rubbed his forehead. "Kyle and Kevin Horner. Their mom went to detox. Ms. Bascomb dropped them off Friday night and picked them up Sunday morning. Took them to an aunt."

"Let me double check."

Gordon heard Lancaster tapping at computer keys. Then the man said, "We have no children named Horner in our system. And no social worker named Bascomb."

"But—"

"I'm sorry, Mr. Trumbull. That's all I can tell you." He hung up, leaving Gordon listening to a dial tone.

Gordon slowly replaced the receiver, wondering if he'd imagined the entire incident. How could a lovely woman and two precious children appear out of nowhere and disappear into the same?

Then he thought of the many mysteries that surrounded the Christmas season. "I guess I'll never know," he murmured. "But it was fun while it lasted."

LEST YE BE JUDGED

Margery Dawes set down her coffee cup and said to her best friend, Jean Winston, "I never have liked that Fred McIlhenny."

"I know just what you mean," Jean replied. "He struts around the neighborhood like he's the king of the street when he walks that Rottweiler of his."

"It's actually a Doberman," Margery corrected, "but Fred acts like he's controlling the Hound of the Baskervilles. Such a smug man."

Jean glanced at the clock on the stove and tucked a gray wisp of hair behind her ear. "Gotta run. My stylist throws a fit if I'm the least little bit late. And I'm getting a perm today. Joe wants me to look my best for our party."

"It's not like the world will end if my hairdresser has to wait a few minutes. It's enough to make me switch salons." Margery patted her teased and sprayed updo. She hadn't changed her style since she and Frank had married.

Jean slipped on her fake fur jacket and walked to the kitchen door. "Thanks for the coffee. See you around six Christmas Eve."

Margery waved as Jean followed the packed path across the snow-covered yard to her house next door. Then she washed the cups and set them in the drainer to dry. As she wiped the counter and table top, she thought about all the things that irritated her: people who ambled through stores, blocking the aisles with their carts; people who broke the speed limit and flipped her off because she stayed a steady five miles under it; checkout clerks who spent more time gossiping with the customers than ringing up sales; kids who used her yard as a shortcut to the woods in summer; and most of all, those who lived off the taxpayers. She didn't believe in welfare and food stamps. If women wanted to have children, they should get married first and make their husbands take care of them. She was particularly peeved that her property taxes went to feed school kids free breakfast and lunch. When she was a kid, her mother had fixed breakfast every day, and she took a sandwich, a waxed paper bag with a few potato chips, and half a package of Twinkies to school for her lunch. "Pure laziness," she muttered as she imagined welfare mothers in sloppy pajama pants (which they also wore shopping!) shunting their little ones out the door for someone else to feed.

Margery went to the living room and put a stack of library books into her Friends of the

Library tote bag. The library would be closed Friday, Saturday, and Sunday this year, because of Christmas. She'd need at least five new books to see her through until Monday.

Losing Frank ten years ago after thirty-eight years of marriage had changed her life drastically, and she hated change. It had taken her a year or better to get used to having no one to cook for, no one to nag about the dirty clothes that missed the hamper or the Sunday paper strewn across the carpet. Sticking to her strict schedule of meals, cleaning, and running errands helped her cope with loneliness, although she called it aloneness. She certainly wasn't going to become one of those weepy widows who depended on other people to keep her occupied and happy.

Her children had already moved away by the time Frank passed. Paul, her son, and Dena, her daughter, lived in separate states halfway across the country. Margery had hoped that they might come home for Christmas this year, but neither of them wanted to travel with their own kids, all under the age of ten.

"Big storm brewing along the coast, Mom," Paul had said when he'd called last week. "I don't want to risk driving a thousand miles in God knows what kind of conditions."

Dena had echoed his sentiments when Margery had called her. "Sorry, Mom. Tom has to work all weekend and I don't want to haul the kids on a plane. But we could send you a plane ticket and you can spend Christmas with us."

Margery had let her voice quiver a bit as she said, "You know I've never been one to roam all over creation. No, I'll just stay home—alone—and have a nice, quiet time." She hung up, feeling smug in her rightness. After all, Dena couldn't really expect her to trundle luggage through airports, make connections, and be stuck for hours—or days—in some dreadful terminal because her flight was delayed. The children should have had enough respect for her to make the effort to come home.

So instead of putting up a tree and decorating the house, she sent presents to the grandchildren, checks to Paul and Dena, and opened the presents they sent the day the mailman delivered them. Christmas dinner would be a baked chicken (most of which would go in the freezer), a small microwaved potato, and store-bought cheesecake for dessert.

Jean was lucky. At least she had Joe. They'd soon celebrate forty-five years of wedded bliss. Their kids, who lived only an hour away, would come home for the holiday, and Jean would invite Margery over on Christmas Eve tomorrow for eggnog (spiked or not, her choice), homemade sugar cookies

164

decorated by tiny fingers, and carols sung to the accompaniment of the out-of-tune piano in Jean's family room. On Christmas Day, Margery would stay in, stay warm, read all day or watch old movies on television, and be content.

She put on her old but still serviceable woolen coat, tied a scarf around her head, tugged on gloves, and picked up her tote bag and purse on the way out the door. A high haze turned the sky pale gray. The wind tossed winter's breath in her face. From the looks of the weather map on TV, they'd have fresh snow for Christmas.

Margery grudgingly paid the boy next door to shovel her sidewalk and driveway every time it snowed. She wished she and George had bought a house with an attached garage, but her late husband had fallen in love with this place just after they married and had ignored her wishes. For the rest of their marriage, he had allowed her to make the big decisions, preferring calm to conflict, and Margery eventually forgave him for making her walk the dozen steps to the garage.

Even though Tim had cleaned the drive just three days ago, a flurry had left a dusting of snow on the drive, so she kept her eyes on the ground, spreading her legs slightly to improve her balance. She certainly didn't need to fall, not at her age. Her mother had never recovered from a broken hip, dying two months later in a nursing home. Margery did not intend to suffer the same fate.

Three feet from the garage door, her left foot hit a patch of ice, hidden by the thin layer of powder, that had formed when snowmelt from the roof trickled onto the drive. Her purse and books flew into the air as the garage tumbled and the sky whirled above her, and then the back of her head hit the ground. She was out cold.

"Mrs. Dawes! Are you all right?" Ginger White, the shoveler's mother, knelt beside Margery, shaking her.

Margery groaned and opened her eyes, then squinted against the light. "What happened?"

"I was looking out the window and saw you fall. I ran right over. Should I call 911?"

Margery struggled to sit up. Ginger pressed a hand to her chest to keep her down. "You shouldn't move until you get checked out. Something might be broken. I'll run home and call. The paramedics can be here in a few minutes."

Margery batted at the hand that held her. "Nonsense. I'm perfectly fine. Or I will be once I get up. Give me a hand. And don't you dare call an ambulance. They charge an arm and a leg just for showing up."

Ginger put an arm under Margery's shoulders and helped her sit up, then helped her to her feet. "Let's get you back in the house," she said, trying to lead Margery back inside.

Margery shook her off. "I have library books to return and groceries to buy. I'll be fine. Thank you." She bent to gather her spilled books and purse contents. Ginger knelt to help.

"If you'd just raise the garage door, I'd appreciate it," Margery said as she dusted snow off her backside. Her fingers experimented with the lump on the back of her head, but snow-wet hair and a bit of tenderness seemed to be the only side effects.

Ginger pulled the door up and Margery got into the car. She backed out, scarcely glancing at Ginger, and drove off.

The library was uncommonly noisy when Margery entered. She remembered when speaking above a whisper was the eighth deadly sin, but things had changed. Now people didn't bother to lower their voices at all. They seemed to have no concept of how disturbing it was to someone who wanted to browse to be surrounded by chatter. But this level of noise was absurd. She scowled at one of the library aides, hoping she'd take the hint and tell the talkers to shut up, but no such luck. She dropped her books on the return counter and walked toward the mysteries. She was a fan of cozies, especially Meg Cabot, but had no use for James Patterson (too vulgar) or Lee Child (too violent), or Lilian Jackson Braun (too vapid).

Passing two rather seedy men sitting at one of the reading tables, she heard one of them say, "Wonder when the soup kitchen opens on Christmas?"

The other said, "I miss my kids. Do they miss me?"

She whirled around and hissed, "Would you please shut up? Some of us come here for peace and quiet."

The long-haired, bearded man looked up at her. "Why don't you shut up? You're the only one making noise."

Margery chuffed and drew herself up. "I distinctly heard you two chattering."

The other man shook his head. "Never said a word, lady. You must be hearing things."

Margery spun on her heel and stalked off, listening to the men discuss her, talking over each other, confusing her. "Old battle axe. Must be loony. Can't get a little rest, even in here." She hurried down the stacks and the men's voices faded, but other mutterings and snickerings tugged at her concentration. She grabbed books from the shelves, hardly paying attention to what she picked. Tucking them into her tote, she stalked toward the check-out, ignoring the racket all around her. Tossing her library card on the desk, she waited impatiently while the clerk scanned them. Then she hurried out of the building, sighing as she reached the relative quiet of the outdoors, the traffic noise a mere murmur after the cacophony in the library.

She drove to the supermarket, parked and went in. The din was even worse than the library. She began to wonder if the fall had affected her hearing, making it more acute. She shook her head, trying to dislodge the fragments of conversation that packed into her brain.

Pushing her shopping cart through the aisles, she filled it with chicken noodle soup, Wonder bread, her Christmas chicken, a bakery cheesecake, and frozen peas and frozen strawberries. By the time she started toward the front of the store, she had heard that a man had been laid off two days ago and was dreading telling his family, that a teenaged girl was trying to decide if she should have sex with her boyfriend for the first time, and a dozen other intimate ramblings that should have remained private.

At the check stand, she tapped her foot impatiently as the checker nattered on with the old man in line ahead of her. She certainly didn't need to hear all the details about his wife's illness. She herself seldom got sick and she would never whine to a stranger about her condition.

Margery began to slap her groceries onto the conveyor belt, hoping the old man would take the hint and get his wallet out and pay. The clerk gave her a dirty look and said, "Now, Mr. Peterson, you tell Lila to take care of herself and we'll see her soon."

"I'll do that," he quavered as he stuck his wallet back in his pocket and shuffled away with his bags.

"Some people ought to have a little compassion, especially at this time of year. Too bad she can't shift about thirty pound of her fat to Miz Peterson. Chemo's about to starve her to death," Margery heard the clerk say.

"If you're speaking to me, young lady, at least have the courtesy to look at me."

The clerk gave her a puzzled look. "I didn't say a word."

Margery's mouth tightened. "You seem to think I don't have any compassion. Well, let me tell you—"

The man behind Margery said, "Lady, you mind moving along? There's other folks want to get home."

"How dare you!"

A woman farther back in the line shouted, "For cryin' out loud, get a move on!"

Margery stared at the people in line. They all stood stoically, avoiding her stare. None of their mouths were moving, even though she distinctly heard their words.

"That'll be twenty-six dollars and thirty-nine cents," the clerk said, putting the Wonder bread in the top of the bag.

Disoriented, Margery handed the clerk two twenties and grabbed the sack without waiting for her change, huffing out of the market to the sound of laughter. In the car, things quieted down. By the time she arrived home, she'd convinced herself that the bump on her head had given her hallucinations.

She had barely unpacked her groceries and put them away before Jean was knocking on the back door. "Ginger told me what happened," Jean gushed. "I think you should go to the emergency room."

"I'm just fine," Margery said. "Want some coffee?"

"Thanks. I'll have a cup." Jean pulled out her usual chair and sat at the table while Margery poured water into the drip coffee maker.

"I wish you hadn't got rid of your percolator." Jean sighed.

"You know it was on its last legs," Margery said.

"What?"

"The percolator. It was falling apart."

Jean swung around to look at Margery. "Of course it was. Why on earth did you bring it up?"

"Oh, never mind." Margery put some mint Milanos on a plate and put them on a tray, along with two coffee mugs and a carton of half and half. She poured coffee and carried the tray to the table.

Jean sipped her coffee. Words blossomed in Margery's head. "Poor Margie. She's losing it. Well, living alone can do that to a person. At least she has us for Christmas Eve."

Margery's cup tilted. Hot liquid splashed onto the table. She jumped up and ran for the sponge by the sink as Jean made little sorry sounds and tried to dab up the spill with her napkin. By the time Margery had the mess cleaned up, she was in control once again. "Don't know what made me so clumsy. Maybe I *am* a little woozy from the fall. I think I'll make an early night of it."

Jean fluttered and flitted, offering to check in on her every hour, to cook her supper, to help.

Margery waved away her concern. "If I need anything I'll call you. And missing a meal or two certainly won't hurt me," she said, patting her stoutness, thinking of the old man and his dying wife. She wished she *could* share some of her health with them both.

After Jean had left, Margery decided to call Dena and tell her what had happened. The phone rang and rang. Just as Margery was ready to hang up, Dena's breathless voice came on.

172

"Hi, Mom."

"How'd you know it was me?"

"Caller I.D. You really need to come out of the Dark Ages, Mom."

Margery snapped, more roughly than she intended, "If I want to know who's calling, I simply pick up the phone and say hello."

"God, I wish she'd lighten up a little," Dena said. Or did she? Margery wondered.

"I just called to tell you I slipped on some ice and fell this afternoon."

"God, Mom, are you okay?" Dena's voice rose to fright pitch.

"Fit as a fiddle." Margery heard the sounds of a scuffle and muffled screams in the background.

"You kids stop it, now!" Dena shouted away from the receiver. Then her voice sounded clearly in Margery's head, but was she really speaking? "I was afraid of this. Mom'll have to go to a home if she can't live alone. And she certainly can't come here! We barely have room for the five of us. And Paul sure wouldn't take her in. Sorry, Mom. The kids are all wound up from visiting Santa. We just got back from the mall."

Margery's hand shook and she had to clear her throat. "I'd better let you get back to whatever you're doing. Just wanted to let you know I'm fine."

"Love you, Mom. I'll call you Christmas

day."

"Love you, too," Margery whispered, hanging up. Either she was going crazy or she had somehow picked up ESP. Whatever was causing it, she didn't like it, not at all. Maybe a good night's sleep would cure her.

Friday morning, Jean came over for coffee as usual. Margery watched her like a dieter counts calories. Jean's thoughts came through to her clearly, the theme seeing to center on "poor Margie": all alone, no real Christmas, coping on her own. After half an hour, Margery was tired of all the pity seeping out of Jean's mind. "I hate to rush you, but I have some errands to do," she said as she pulled the plate of cookies out of Jean's reach just as her neighbor started to take another. "I'll see you tomorrow night for the sing-along."

"Oh. Sure." Jean carried her cup to the sink and went to the door. "Come early if you want to. The kids will be here by noon, and we can party hearty."

Margery snickered. Partying at Jean's house meant an extra serving of eggnog and cranking up the volume on the singing. She kept her expression pleasant as she said, "Can't wait."

She drove to her favorite coffee shop and went inside, taking her place in line behind a young man who nodded pleasantly to her before placing his order. Somehow his smile seemed to hold her as a father holds a baby. Before she could return his cknowledgement, he walked away.

The counter girl smiled and said, "What can I get for you?"

"A small latté, black."

Geez, lady. Why don't you learn to order right? You want a damn cup of coffee, not a latté. The girl continued smiling as she took Margery's money. "You can pick up your order at the end of the counter. Merry Christmas," she said as she handed Margery her change.

The couple behind Margery shouldered her aside, eager to place their order, and she went to pick up her coffee. The barista was just putting the finishing touches on a cup for the man ahead of Margery, pouring steamed milk on top of the coffee in his cup and swirling it into a heart shape. "Here's your latté, sir," the girl said as she handed it to him. Then she poured a cup of black coffee from an insulated pitcher and handed it to Margery. "Merry Christmas, ma'am," she said, smiling.

Margery took the cup to a corner table and sat down, stunned. When the fancy names for coffee had come along, she adopted the lingo, feeling sophisticated. All this time she'd thought she was ordering the right thing. Now it turned out to be wrong, so wrong. What else had she been wrong about in her life? Her hand trembled as she lifted the cup. Suddenly all the things she'd been so sure of seemed to totter on a precipice.

She left the cup barely tasted and rose to leave, accidentally bumping the arm of a man at the next table. He scowled, his lips tight. *Clumsy cow. Watch what you're doing.*

Margery blushed as she answered his unspoken criticism. "I'm so sorry. Please excuse me." She rushed to the door and almost ran to the car. Barely paying attention as she backed out of the parking space, she heard tires screech, a horn blare, and a jumble of words: *Crap's sake! That old bat almost hit me!* She put the car into drive and sped toward the safety of her living room.

On Saturday, Margery ventured out again, this time to the mall. As she crossed the parking lot, voices shouted around her. Inside Target the din rose to an unbearable level. Margery turned and ran back to her car. She drove downtown and parked in the city lot that took up half a block behind a row of shops.

She strolled to Main Street and began walking, bracing herself for the tumult of sound to assault her, but only murmured words came to her, mostly about presents, holiday decorations, and other signs of the season. She wondered if she could tune in to thoughts people had about others, not just about her. Cautiously, she opened her mind.

A woman tugging a little boy by the hand strode past. "Slow down, Mom," the little boy said, and Margery saw his mouth move, so she knew he was actually speaking.

The mother's mouth didn't' move. *We've got to get to the shelter before they run out of room. Too cold in the car last night. We need a warm bed, even if we have to share. Why the hell did Dave leave us? He knew I couldn't keep up the house payment, not without child support. Fat chance of getting any of that!*

Margery stopped and stared as they hustled down the street. Homeless at Christmas! What a shame. More thoughts rushed at her: a father who had spent his week's pay on presents and now didn't have enough to pay the utility bill; an old woman, eyes vacant, whose thoughts were so jumbled that Margery could make no sense of them; a couple who were so angry at each other that she jerked her mind away from their thoughts of mayhem and revenge. Suffering rushed at her from all sides.

Then in the midst of the misery, a man's voice spoke. *As you sow, so shall you reap.* Margery looked around but saw no one who looked as if the words had come from him. The voice spoke again. *Change your thinking, change your life.*

"Where are you? *Who* are you?" Margery said aloud.

I speak to your heart. A heart sore with grief and outrage, a heart that longs for peace.

Tears trembled on Margery's lashes. The voice had cut to the quick of her being, and now the fears that she'd tried to bury with years of judgment roiled inside, a tornado of torment.

A hand touched her shoulder. The young man who had stood in line at the coffee shop stood beside her, radiating goodwill and kindness through his fingertips. "Lady, are you all right?"

Margery cleared her throat, wondering where he had come from. "I feel a bit dizzy," she admitted.

He took her arm and led her to a bench outside a carpet store. "Sit for a minute. I'll get you some water." He disappeared inside and came back in a minute with a paper cup. "Drink this. It may help." He sat beside her as he handed her the cup.

Margery drank half the water, then breathed deeply, trying to quiet her mind. "Thank you. I'm feeling a bit better," she said.

The young man leaned closer, smiling, his eyes full of love. "Face your fears and you will find there is nothing to fear." It was the voice she had heard just before he touched her.

Her voice quavered. "Why are you picking on me?"

His voice filled her head, his lips still. *I'm picking up, not on. It's time to let the healing begin.* He stood up, tucking his hands in his pockets, and gave her a look of such joy and affection that she began to weep again. He laid a hand on her head. "Go in peace, he said. And then he was gone.

Margery drove home in a daze, his words racing around in her mind. As she neared the house, an unfamiliar lightness filled her, as if all her worries were drifting off through the top of her head. She went inside and lay down, falling into a sleep without dreams.

She woke hours later, clear headed and happy, and freshened up. She almost skipped across the yard to Jean's house, where Christmas lights blazed and the sound of the piano drifted into the night.

Jean pressed a spiked eggnog into Margery's hand as Joe took her coat and hung it up. "Merry Christmas," he shouted.

Laughter surrounded her, and she found herself chuckling at the knock-knock jokes Jean's grandkids insisted on telling. Through the uproar she could pick up crumbs of thoughts: the presents the kids wanted Santa to bring, Jean's and Joe's joy at seeing the family gathered together, bits and pieces of dinner plans, presents to be hauled out of hiding when the children were asleep.

Then Joe's voice overrode the others. "Margie sure looks different tonight. Acts different, too. Wonder what happened to change her?"

She grinned at him. "You wouldn't believe me if I told you."

"Huh?"

"Never mind," she said, holding out her empty cup. "Fill 'er up, please." And Joe hurried to obey.

By New Year's Eve Margery had learned to really see the people she met and to take them as they were, not as how she thought they should be. The more she opened up to the differences around her, the fainter the voices in her head became, until somewhere around mid-February they vanished for good.

Still, Margery's new way of seeing the world and the people in it continued. Grassy patches spread as snow melted. Crocuses, purple and yellow and gold, decorated March. Tree buds swelled with new leaves. On the day the first robin appeared, Margery felt winter fall away from her soul, and rejoiced.

LOST AND FOUND

Katherine Malloy frowned and shook her head as another splotch of turkey gravy landed on her apron. If it were up to her, the vagrants and bums who crowded into the local soup kitchen for Thanksgiving dinner could starve—or get a job. She'd worked hard all her life, ever since she'd left home the day after she'd graduated from high school. No matter where she'd found herself, she'd always managed to eat and put a roof over her head.

She barely glanced at the bearded man who held out his plate eagerly, grinning at her with a mouth twelve teeth shy of a full smile. Without speaking or acknowledging him in any way, she dolloped gravy on his turkey and mashed potatoes.

Thank you, ma'am," he said.

She ignored the pleasantry and held out her ladle toward the next plate.

Spending Thanksgiving at the local soup kitchen had definitely not been on her Christmas list. She'd planned to dine at Le Table d'Or, one of the most exclusive restaurants in town. She hadn't cooked a turkey in her life and didn't plan to do so anytime soon. In fact, she didn't even like turkey and the thought of stuffing bread, celery, onions, and spices into a dead bird and eating it six hours later made her queasy.

She continued ladling out the holiday while her mind wandered back to the meeting that had ended up with her here instead of dining on duck l'orange and wild rice. The Monday morning meeting at Powell and Smythe had begun as all the others before. Then Mr. Powell had thrown the curve ball that caught her squarely in her ambition.

"As you know, Powell and Smythe supports many charitable causes, but charity is more than just writing a check now and again. Our corporate mission includes more than just profit and loss. We are part of a larger community and as part of that community I urge each of you to give back in some way." He held out a paper. "I have here a sign-up sheet for volunteering to serve at the local soup kitchen from now until Christmas. The company has committed for one employee a day to work from eleven until two, whether it be cooking, serving, or washing up. We can make the community a better place and feel the satisfaction of doing something to help those less fortunate. Of course, you'll be paid for the time you're away from your desk."

Katherine refrained from rolling her eyes at his platitudes. She'd do her damnedest to keep from ladling up slop for transients and weirdos. The paper made its way around the room. Katherine passed it to the woman next to her. As the clipboard left her hand, she caught Mr. Powell's eye. He raised his eyebrows. She kept her face impassive.

When the list came back to him, he scanned it. "We have almost one hundred percent cooperation. There's only one slot left." He raised his eyes and looked into hers.

Flushing, she stared back.

Mr. Powell's smile, produced to induce an atmosphere of cooperation, faded. "I'll e-mail a copy of the assignments to you so you can plan accordingly. Thank you all for your help in giving a bit of yourselves to others." He walked out of the room, glancing as Katherine as he passed, his expression somewhere between disappointment and disdain.

She dropped her eyes, suddenly feeling as if she had failed some unwritten test. As she followed the other employees out, she wished she had taken her turn, even though the idea of being within a few feet of dirty, smelly people gave her the willies.

Jocelyn, the office manager, caught up with Katherine. "Which day did you sign up for?" she asked.

Katherine shrugged. "I didn't."

Jocelyn's laugh tinkled down the hall. "I wouldn't have had the nerve to say no. You're lucky you're high enough on the totem pole to get away with disobeying a direct order, even if it's phrased as a request." She laughed again. "Oh, well. It won't kill me to do a good deed once in a while, as long as I still get paid." She bounced off, her hair swinging, leaving Katherine to her thoughts.

By the end of the day, she had reconsidered her attitude. Even though Powell hadn't ordered them to volunteer (it wouldn't be volunteering if one were conscripted), she had sensed his disappointment, and letting one of the firm's principals down was probably not the best way to continue her climb to partner in the investment firm. She slipped on her coat and started toward the elevator. As she passed Mr. Powell's office, he came out, nearly running her down.

"Sorry," he said.

"Actually, I was just coming to see you. I'd like to sign up for soup kitchen detail." She smiled at his look of surprise.

"Certainly. There's one spot left. I assume that will be all right?"

She nodded. "Glad to do my part for the community."

So here she stood, her head and feet aching, wondering if the line that still stretched out the door would ever come to an end or if they'd run out of food and be able to shut down the operation.

A woman herded two children, a boy about twelve and a girl around ten, ahead of her. The children held out their plates, eyes downcast as if they were ashamed to be here. Katherine felt a momentary pang at their youth and embarrassment. She smiled as she dished up potatoes and gravy, but they didn't look up. "Thank you, ma'am," the boy said, so softly she almost didn't hear him.

"You're welcome," she replied.

The woman, who must have been their mother, held out her plate and Katherine served her. The woman stood tall and looked her in the eye as she thanked her.

Katherine felt a shiver go through her as she looked into the stranger's eyes. Before she could respond, the woman turned and followed her children to a table in the far corner of the room. Katherine shrugged. There couldn't possibly be anything familiar about that woman. She dismissed the eerie feeling the woman had caused and went on dishing out dinners. As the line dwindled, she glanced around and was surprised to find the woman staring at her. A latecomer held out his plate and Katherine dished out the last dollop of gravy. When she looked up again, the little family was gone.

At last the food was gone, stomachs were filled, and she could go home and put her feet up. She put on her coat and went out to the

185

parking lot. Clouds had gathered as she'd worked, and sleet stung her cheeks as she walked to her Audi. She ducked her head against the icy wind.

A woman's voice brought her up short. "Kathy!"

She whirled around. No one had called her by her childhood nickname for over twenty-five years. The woman who had stared at her so strangely inside was now hurrying toward her. The two children were nowhere in sight.

As the woman drew closer, Katherine squinted at her. Something about the shape of the cheekbones and the eyes jiggled a memory loose. The woman's next words confirmed her suspicions.

"Kathy? It's Norrie." The woman reached toward Katherine.

Katherine's vision darkened and she willed herself not to faint. Blinking back tears, she took the woman's hand. "Oh, my God! How did you—where have you—" She floundered to a stop.

Nora began to cry. "Oh, sis, I never thought I'd see you again!" She threw her arms around Katherine and wept in earnest.

Katherine patted her on the back, struggling to understand how a sister she hadn't seen for over twenty years had managed to track her down. Nora had been only seven when Katherine said goodbye to their controlling parents and, with one suitcase, set off to find her way in the world. A scholarship had allowed her to get two years of a business degree under her belt, and she had worked the night shift as a hospital admittance clerk to save money to pay for the rest of her MBA. It hadn't been easy but she had done it, and her lifestyle, so different from her childhood, reflected her success.

Nora, so much younger, was barely a blip on her radar. Katherine was already in middle school when the new baby came along. By the time she was ready to graduate, Nora had just finished second grade. Since they'd never been close, she'd had no more qualms about leaving her little sister behind than she had leaving her emotionally abusive father and passive mother.

Norrie was back in her life, and what was she to do with her? She stepped back and looked at her sister, who was beaming at her through her tears. "How on earth did you recognize me?" she asked.

"It's too cold to talk out here. Let's get in my car," Nora said, taking Katherine's hand and leading her toward a decade-old minivan. As they neared the car, the boy and girl clambered over the seat to the rear, leaving the front seat empty. Still in shock, Katherine got into the passenger's seat as Nora hurried around to the driver's side. Katherine looked over her shoulder at the kids. They sat with fear-tinged eyes, crowded into a space barely big enough for them. The rest of the van was filled with a jumble of bags, boxes, and clothing.

Nora slammed the door and started the engine. Faint warmth seeped from the vents. "Kathy, this is your nephew, Ben, and your niece, Carrie. Kids, this is your Aunt Kathy."

"Katherine," she automatically corrected.

They murmured hello. Then Carrie said, "How come we never saw her before?"

Ben shot an elbow into his sister's ribs and muttered, "Don't be rude. Remember what Mom said."

Katherine extended a hand over the seat. "I'm pleased to meet you," she said as little hands briefly took hers. Then she turned to Nora. "Are you living here in town?"

Nora chuckled. "You might say that. Home is where the van is." A flicker of pain crossed her face, quickly erased by a smile. "It's a long story. Sure you have time?"

Katherine, appalled, was silent for a moment. Then she said, "Look. I live not far from here. Why don't you follow me and we can catch up in comfort." She opened the van door and stepped out. "I'm driving the gray Audi."

On the fifteen-minute drive to her house, Katherine wondered what she had gotten herself into. Would Nora and the kids want to live with her? Should she offer to let them stay?

What if they never went away? She couldn't envision kids tearing through her carefully, and expensively, furnished home. And what would Charles think of her instant family? She and he had been casually dating for six months, long enough for intimacy, not long enough for the exchange of house keys.

When they arrived at the house, she drove into the attached garage. Nora pulled into the drive and shut off the van. As they got out, Katherine pointed to the door leading from the garage into the kitchen. "Welcome to my humble abode."

As they entered, the two children shivered involuntarily as heat surrounded them. Nora shrugged out of her threadbare woolen pea coat and took the kids' coats. "Where shall I hang them?"

Katherine held out her arms for them. "I'll take them. Make yourselves comfortable. The living room's through there," she said nodding as she walked through the state-of-the-art kitchen. Stainless steel gleamed and the marble island reflected the track lights. By the time she'd hung the coats in the hall closet, Nora and her children had moved into the living room, sitting on the edge of the couch, as if they were afraid to get too comfortable. They had left their shoes at the back door. Two of Ben's toes stuck out of his right sock.

Katherine pushed a button on the gas fireplace and flames climbed artificial logs, brightening the room and radiating more heat into it. She kicked off her shoes and curled up in the oversized armchair that was her favorite. "Now tell me everything, Norrie."

As her sister talked, Katherine got an idea of what her life had been like. Nora had married her high school sweetheart almost as soon as they graduated. Ben had come along a year later, Carrie two years after that. Unfortunately, Nora's husband had been a clone of their father, shouting at Nora and the kids, blaming them for all his failures. Finally, when the economy tanked, he had taken off, leaving their home in foreclosure and child support only a pipe dream. For almost a year now, Nora and the kids had been living in their van, washing in gas station restrooms, cooking on a gas camping stove, sometimes sleeping outside on the grass if the weather was warm enough.

Katherine's eyes glistened. "Hang on, Norrie. Let's have something to drink. Kids? I have diet Coke or root beer or Sprite."

The two had relaxed a bit as Nora narrated her short autobiography. Now they sat up straight again. "Root beer, please," Carrie said, and Ben nodded.

In a few minutes Katherine came back with a tray holding the sodas with glasses full of ice, two goblets of merlot, and a bowl of snack crackers accompanied by a plate of cheese. She set the tray on the coffee table in front of the couch, handed Nora a glass of wine, took hers and retreated to her chair. She nodded for Nora to continue.

Her sister swept her dark hair behind her ears and went on. "I pick up temp jobs here and there, and last summer I worked at Burger King in Springfield. Sales slowed down once the weather changed and I got riffed." At Katherine's glance, she explained, "Reduction in force. So we headed south and heard an ad on the radio for a free dinner. And you know the rest."

Katherine stared at her sister, whom she remembered as a child, but who had turned into one of those transients that she so resented. "Of course you'll stay here," she said, setting down her glass on the raised hearth.

The kids looked at each other, then at their mother, as though they couldn't believe what they had heard. Nora flushed. "We didn't come here to beg for charity," she said, her voice tight.

Katherine waved the words away. "You're family, for heaven's sake! I'm certainly not going to send you out into the storm. Kids, why don't you go get some of your clothes out of the van?"

Ben and Carrie jumped up, joy shining from

their eyes. "Can we, Mom? Huh? Can we?" Ben urged.

Nora nodded, her eyes on the floor. As soon as they had scurried out of the room, she turned to Katherine. "But only for a few days. And we won't be in your way."

Katherine realized that even blood ties couldn't overcome years of separation in an instant. Deep in her conscience, a feeling of relief stirred. She wouldn't be stuck with them forever. She nodded. "Whatever you like."

Two nights later, after the kids were in bed, Katherine and Nora sat in front of the fire, sipping wine and talking. Nora had said little about what her childhood was like, turning away Katherine's questions. "You know. You were there," was her only reply.

Tears welled in Katherine's eyes as she looked at her baby sister who had gone through so much since they'd last seen each other. She looked back to the flames, swallowing hard. "Norrie, I'm so sorry I left you. If I hadn't been so young and self-centered—"

"You did what you had to do. You saved yourself," Nora replied. She went on before Katherine could answer. "It wasn't so bad. I learned to hide out when Dad went on a rampage. I spent a lot of time at the library and with friends." She drank deeply. "I just don't understand why I couldn't see Dad in my husband. I thought Harvey really loved me and just wanted to keep me to himself. I felt safe with him, at least for the first couple of years. When he ran out on us, my first thought was 'I'm free! Finally free!' I should have left him years ago but didn't have the guts. And even as hard as it's been since, I have absolutely no regrets."

Katherine finished her wine and reached for the bottle, topping off both glasses. They sat in silence for a long time.

* * * * *

On Monday, Katherine came home from work, tired and cross. One of her clients had withdrawn his account, leaving her scrambling to explain the loss to Mr. Powell, which was hard to do as she had no idea why. By four o'clock, one of her rare migraines threatened. All she wanted to do was to get home, take a long bath, and go to bed.

The aroma of meatloaf made her stomach churn as she opened the kitchen door to see Nora stirring a pot of potatoes. "Hi, Kathy. I hope you don't mind that I started dinner."

"Thanks," she said, her tone sharp as she massaged her temples. She hadn't had meatloaf and mashed potatoes since she'd left home. As she passed her sister, she saw Nora's expression falter, guilt replacing excitement.

The kids were in the living room, watching television. A chenille throw lay crumpled on the couch. Papers and pencils were scattered on the coffee table. A pair of socks lay draped over the back of the armchair. To her orderly mind, the place looked like a tornado had ripped through.

"Hi, Aunt Kathy," Carrie said.

"Pick up this mess right now!" Katherine snapped as she hung up her coat.

Ben hit the remote to turn off the TV and began to shuffle the papers into a stack. Carrie grabbed the socks and headed for the guest room where she and Nora were sleeping. Ben folded the throw, laying it neatly on the couch before he fled, clutching the papers and pencils to his chest.

Katherine went into her bathroom and swallowed a couple of pain relievers, hoping they would block the ache in her head. As she walked back to the living room, Nora appeared in the doorway, wiping her hands on a towel. "Dinner will be ready in about half an hour. Where are the kids? I thought they were in here."

Katherine rubbed her aching temples, praying for the meds to kick in. "I'm not hungry. I'm going out. Don't wait up." She put her coat back on, brushing past Nora, heading for the garage. She slammed the kitchen door and pulled her cell out of her purse. As she waited for the garage door to rise in response to the push button on her dash, she dialed Charles' number. He answered on the second ring. "Can I come over?" she asked, her voice breaking.

"Sure. Want to go out to eat?" he said.

"Wait until I get there." She snapped the phone shut and gunned out of the garage into the street, tires squealing.

* * * * *

Sitting on Charles' couch, his arm around her, she felt the tension begin to leave her and the pain in her head had dwindled from agony to inconvenience. She'd given him a succinct recap of her weekend and first day back at work. He'd poured her a scotch on the rocks and commiserated. "The worst part is she's my sister. I can't kick her out, not when she's down and out," Katherine said.

"Mmmm," he murmured, letting his hand caress her breast through her work dress. "Why don't we sleep on it? Things'll be clearer in the morning."

She lifted her face to kiss him, then nuzzled his neck. He stood and led the way to the bedroom.

* * * * *

In spite of the scotch and sex, Katherine didn't sleep well. Guilt plagued her whenever she remembered the looks on Ben's and Carrie's faces as they scuttled away from her temper. She wondered if they had told Nora how she had treated them. She'd have to apologize. It was the first time in years that she had had to

195

account for her actions to anyone but her bosses and herself, and she didn't like the feeling. She'd start looking in the rental section of the paper. Getting Norrie and the kids into a place of their own would be worth the expense.

At last dawn tinted the shades and she roused herself to shower. She'd have to go home and change. She couldn't show up at work in yesterday's clothes. It wouldn't send the right message to management. She sighed and stepped under the steaming stream of water.

When she arrived home, Nora and the kids were still asleep. She dressed quickly and quietly and slipped out of the house undetected. Just ten minutes after arriving, she was gone again.

* * * * *

All day she wondered what she'd find when she got home. Her heart beat faster as she pulled up to the house and saw Nora's van sitting in the driveway. She trudged inside, ready to face whatever wrath Nora might wreak on her.

Nora and the kids were in the living room, watching TV. Nora smiled at Katherine. "Guess what? I got a job!"

Katherine tried to smile back. "That's great! Tell all." She tossed her coat on the back of the armchair and sat down. Ben and Carrie scooted closer to each other on the couch and eyed her warily. Guilt struck her again.

"I saw a help wanted sign at Lucille's Diner. I went in and they hired me on the spot."

"What will you be doing?"

"Waitressing. I used to do it part time when Harvey and I were first married. I'm pretty darned good, if I do say so myself." She leaned forward, staring at Katherine intently. "If tips are good, we can move in to our own place before Christmas. I checked out a couple of apartments while I was running around. There's a one-bedroom that we can get really cheap."

"I could loan you the first and last month's rent and you could move in any time," Katherine said, relieved that she wouldn't have to do any house hunting. If Nora took her up on the offer she could spend the holidays with Charles.

Nora drew back. "We'll manage. I don't want to owe anyone anything."

Katherine stifled a sigh. She wanted her home to herself. Was that so wrong?

"I'll just go clean up the kitchen," Nora said, leaving Katherine alone with the kids.

Katherine cleared her throat. "Ben, Carrie, I owe you an apology for blowing up at you the way I did. I'm sorry."

"That's okay." Ben took Carrie's hand.

197

"Let's go do our homework." They stood up, expressions still wary, and left their aunt wondering if they had really forgiven her outburst. She sighed. Once broken, trust was hard to restore.

By the second week, the stress of having people around all the time was telling on Katherine. Even though the kids now kept messes confined to their rooms, they still seemed to tiptoe around their aunt, finding excuses to disappear whenever she came in. She began to stay later at the office and stop at restaurants for dinner on the way home.

* * * * *

On a Thursday in mid-December, Nora came home from work and said, "Tips have been really good this week, and I think Ben and Carrie need a night out. They want to see that new Pixar movie. We'll go out for pizza before. You'll have the house to yourself tomorrow evening."

Katherine's heart jumped. "Have a great time," she said, already planning a long bath and a book in bed. Or maybe she'd have Charles over for an intimate dinner. Suddenly the possibilities seemed endless.

* * * * *

Katherine hurried home from work Friday night, eager to relax with a glass of wine and the early news before submerging herself in chin-deep hot water and scented oil. Charles had turned down her invitation to come over. "Sorry, honey. Got a late meeting and I have no idea when it will be over. The kids will probably be back before I get away." Katherine wondered what kind of meeting would last until ten on a Friday night but decided a bath and a book would be a nice change of pace.

When she arrived at the house, she was surprised to see Nora's van still there. She hurried inside, where a wan Nora sat at the kitchen table. Ben waited for a tea kettle to boil. Carrie sat beside her mother and patted her hand.

Nora looked up. "Looks like our plans are on hold," she rasped, blotting red and puffy eyes with a tissue.

Carrie's brow furrowed. "Mama's got a cold."

Ben poured hot water over a teabag, and a scent of peppermint floated through the kitchen. He set the cup in front of his mother. "Here, Mom. This will make you feel better."

"I'm so sorry," Katherine said. "Anything I can do to help?"

"Nothing. Except, would you mind fixing the kids something to eat?" Nora's head dropped forward as she coughed.

Ben said, "We don't need to bother Aunt Katherine. I can make some mac and cheese and do the dishes. Then Carrie and I can go in my room and read or something."

Katherine smiled at the kids. "I have a better idea. I've been wanting to see that movie myself. And I haven't had pizza in a coon's age."

Carrie clapped her hands and said, "Can we, Mom?"

Ben stepped behind his mother and put his hands on her shoulders. "I don't think we ought to, Carrie. Mom might need us." His expression said that it wasn't only his mother he was worried about.

Nora put down the teacup and gave Katherine a grateful look. "I'll be fine. Just need some sleep. You kids go on and have a good time. You can tell me all about it tomorrow. Go get your coats."

The children left, Carrie eagerly, Ben reluctantly. He kept glancing back at his mother and aunt.

"You sure you don't mind?" Nora said as she stood.

"Not a bit. You get a good night's sleep. I'll just go change out of my work clothes."

In ten minutes, Katherine was dressed in jeans, knee-high boots and a crimson sweater that cost more than a month's rent for the kinds of places Nora had been looking at. As she passed her sister's room, she saw Nora already in the sweat pants and shirt that passed for pajamas, heavy socks on her feet.

"We'll be quiet when we get home," she promised.

Nora coughed and nodded. "Have a good time. Sorry to such a bother."

"Just get better." Katherine closed the door and went into the kitchen. Ben and Carrie were waiting by the back door. Ben's skittish look had mellowed a bit and Carrie practically beamed. Katherine grabbed her purse and car keys. "I know a great pizza place," she said.

* * * * *

She and the kids were still laughing over the movie when they go home. Katherine had been surprised to find out how much she liked it. And how much she enjoyed feeling like a kid again. As they got out of the car, she put a finger to her lips. "Let's let your mom sleep."

Ben and Carrie crept into the house. "Carrie can sleep with me," Ben whispered. "Then she won't have to disturb Mom."

"Good idea," Katherine whispered back. "Where are your pajamas?" she murmured to her niece.

"In Mom's room." Carrie took her coat off and hung it over a kitchen chair, then crept off to get her nightclothes.

"Thanks, Aunt Katherine," Ben said softly. "It was really fun."

She hugged him and he hugged her back. They'd scarcely broken apart when Carrie reappeared. "Aunt Katherine, you better come. Mom's breathing really funny."

Katherine ran down the hall, the children right behind. She bent to touch her sister's forehead. It took only a brief touch to know that Nora was more ill than she had let on. She turned to the kids. "I'm taking her to the hospital. Ben, watch Carrie."

Ben's face was ashen as he gripped his sister's hand. "Can we come, too?"

Katherine bit her lower lip. "All right. Get your coats on and put a pillow in the backseat." They scampered off to do her bidding. She shook Nora. "Wake up, sis. I'm taking you to the emergency room."

Nora roused. "Too tired. Wanna stay here." She started to turn over but Katherine put her arms around her and hauled her up to sit on the edge of the bed.

As the blankets slipped off, Nora began to shiver uncontrollably. Her teeth chattered as Katherine pulled her to her feet. "Lean on me." Together they stumbled down the hall and through the kitchen.

Carrie held the garage door open as Ben hurried to open the Audi's backseat door. He got in and helped Katherine lay Nora on the seat.

"Carrie, get in front. Ben, stay back there and keep your mom from falling off."

"She's shaking awful hard. Shouldn't we

put a blanket over her?" he said.

Katherine started the car and began to pull out of the garage. "She's got a high fever. The cold air will help bring it down. Just hang on to her." Her knuckles were white on the wheel as she tried to still the shaking that was almost as bad as Nora's.

* * * * *

The ER waiting room was noisy and crowded. Katherine sat with the kids, one on either side, waiting for the doctor to finish examining Nora in one of the curtained cubicles.

"Will she be all right?" Ben asked.

"Sure," Katherine said. "This hospital is one of the best in the state. If they can't fix her, nobody can."

"God can." Tears slipped down Carrie's face, in spite of her brave words.

Katherine put an arm around her. "I'm sure we won't have to bother him. The doctors know what they're doing." Carrie leaned against her and closed her eyes. Katherine pulled her closer. In the three weeks they'd been at the house, Nora had not shown any signs of wanting to go to church. Of course, on two Sundays she'd been scheduled to work at the diner. The children had not said anything about Sunday school, but she'd once passed by Ben's room as he knelt, hands folded, eyes closed, lips moving silently. She assumed that Nora and

Carrie followed the same routine each night, but she had no idea what church—or churches—they might have attended.

It was after midnight when the doctor came out and called, "Katherine Malloy?"

"Here." She stood up. Carrie and Ben leapt to their feet, reaching for her hands, seeking comfort.

He beckoned and they followed him to a quiet alcove. "I'm afraid your sister's condition is very grave," he said. "We've sent her to ICU. You may visit, but the children cannot. Here's the room number. There's a waiting room near the unit." He handed her a slip of paper. "Sorry to rush off but more patients are waiting."

Katherine led the children to an elevator and punched the button for the floor where the intensive care unit was located. Ben had his arm around Carrie as she sniffled. Katherine took a tissue out of her purse and handed it to the girl. The door opened and they went down the hall to the ICU waiting room.

"Stay here. I'll go check on your mom. I'll be back in a minute." She hurried away and pushed through the doors into the intensive care unit. The nurses' station filled the middle of the room and the patient rooms radiated from the core like spokes on a wheel. Every room was in full view. Behind the desk, nurses monitored banks of blinking, beeping machines.

"I'm Katherine Malloy. My sister, Nora Petty, was admitted a bit ago, and the ER doctor said I could see her."

The nurse got up and led Katherine to a dimly lit room. More monitors blinked and beeped near the bed. Nora lay unmoving. Bottles of fluid hung on either side of the bed; tubes ran into veins in each of her arms. A respirator pulsed quietly, driving oxygen through a tube that had been inserted into her mouth and taped in place. "She's one sick little lady," the nurse murmured.

Katherine's breath caught. "Will she be all right?"

The nurse replied, "I can't give you that information. Dr. Cryder will be making round shortly. He can tell you more. You can have five minutes with her now."

Katherine stood beside the bed as the nurse left, watching Nora's chest rise and fall to the rhythm of the respirator. Tears gathered in her eyes. Had she found her sister only to lose her so swiftly? "Don't die. Please don't die," she whispered. "Ben and Carrie need you. / need you." She touched Nora's forehead, which seemed a bit cooler. Then she went back to the waiting room.

Dr. Cryder wasn't much more hopeful than the nurse. He called Katherine into the hallway outside the waiting room. "I wish I had better news," he said. "Ms. Petty is suffering from a particularly virulent strain of pneumonia—not contagious—but one that is resistant to medications. We'll keep her hydrated and hope that she has the strength to fight off the infection."

"If it's a matter of money—" Katherine began.

Dr. Cryder interrupted her with a raised hand. "We provide care for whoever needs it, regardless of ability to pay." He glanced at Ben and Carrie, who hovered in the doorway. "Take the children home. If anything changes, we'll notify you right away." With that, he turned and hurried away.

"Come on, kids. Let's go home." Katherine shepherded the two out of the hospital.

Ben and Carrie sat in the back seat, and Katherine could hear their mumbled conversation. She tried to understand the words, but they spoke too softly. The way home led past Charles's house, and she glanced at it as they passed. To her surprise the lights were on. She slowed as the front door opened. Charles and a woman came out. The woman turned and Charles kissed her. It was obvious from the way she molded herself to him that this wasn't a casual—or a first time—occurrence. "That must have been one helluva business meeting," she muttered as she sped away.

* * * * *

Carrie and Ben had gone to bed and Katherine sat curled on the couch, watching the flames from the fireplace dance shadows across the room. Her wine glass was still almost full. She'd been too lost in thought to do more than sip. Her thoughts ricocheted between Nora and Charles. To her surprise, Charles's betrayal left her feeling relieved. She realized that they had never been in love and would never have been. Their connection was about sex, fancy dinners, and not much else. A feeling of freedom swept over her.

The flickering flames lulled her into a trance-like state. Before she knew it, she had moved into a dream. In the dream she found herself in Nora's hospital room, seeming to hang in a corner of the ceiling. Below she saw her sister, comatose, her breath barely lifting the sheet covering her. The monitors whispered their messages of pulse, respirations, and other medical information.

A nurse wearing Spongebob-decorated scrubs walked in, examined the monitors, adjusted the IV in Nora's right arm, and went back to her station. Then another figure walked in. The woman wore a mid-calf white dress, reminiscent of nurses a hundred years ago. A starched, white cap was pinned to her hair. As the woman approached Nora, she began to radiate a gentle golden glow. Her right hand touched Nora's forehead, and Nora's body seemed to absorb the light, drawing it in as an unwatered garden soaks up gentle rain.

Katherine lost track of time as she watched the flow of light into Nora's ravaged body. Suddenly the light faded, as did the figure, and with an upward glance at Katherine's hovering form, the mysterious nurse disappeared.

Katherine woke on the couch as dawn lightened the sky. Her neck was stiff, her eyes gritty. She stretched to her feet and started down the hall to her bedroom, stopping to look in on Carrie and Ben, who still slept. After slipping out of her clothes and into a pair of sweats she went to the kitchen and brewed a pot of coffee, puzzling over the remnants of the dream. For it had to have been a dream.

As she poured her first cup, the phone rang. She jumped to answer it. "Hello?"

"This is Dr. Cryder."

Katherine's heart hammered. Was this the news she'd dreaded since yesterday?

"I wanted to let you know that we've moved Ms. Petty out of ICU to a regular room. She's made a remarkable recovery."

"Thank God!" Katherine sank into a chair, tears stinging her eyes. As she listened to the doctor, she was also aware that Ben and Carrie had entered the kitchen and stood, wide-eyed and frightened, across from her. She smiled to reassure them and said goodbye to the doctor.

"Your mom's just fine," she said, and the children burst into tears.

Ben wiped his eyes on his sleeve. "When can we go see her?"

"Just as soon as we get dressed and have some breakfast," Katherine replied.

Forty-five minutes later, they pulled into the hospital parking lot.

* * * * *

Nora was sitting up, sipping tea, when they arrived. The IVs had been removed from her arms, and the children ran to her, one on each side of the bed. She hugged them mightily and kissed them. "Did you miss me?"

"You bet!" Ben said. "We prayed all the way home last night."

Carrie broke in. "We asked God to make you better, and He did!"

Katherine doubted God's role in saving Nora, choosing to believe in antibiotics and medical skill instead. Then a memory of last night's dream flashed through her mind.

Nora spoke. "I had the strangest dream. As least, I think it was a dream. I was so wiped out I couldn't tell what was real."

"What did you dream, Mama?" Carrie asked snuggling closer.

"Well, it was late at night. I couldn't see anything or hear anything. Then I felt a

209

hand touch me. It felt like it was sending love all through me. I managed to open my eyes just a bit and a nurse stood there. She wore a long white dress and a white nurse's cap on her head, like a nurse from the past."

Katherine jumped up. "And she glowed all over and touched you and you began to glow!"

Nora gave her a puzzled look. "Yes, she glowed. And that's when I began to feel better."

"She was an angel!" Ben exclaimed.

"Don't be—" Katherine began to say "ridiculous" but the memory of her dream— or vision—stopped her.

A new doctor came in. "Hi. I'm Dr. Wellcup." He looked over Nora's chart. "You're somewhat of a miracle, you know," he said. "None of us has ever seen anyone throw off this pneumonia the way you did last night. I think another couple of days in the hospital, just to be sure, and then you can go home for Christmas."

* * * * *

On Christmas Eve day, Katherine and the kids picked up Nora, who was waiting eagerly. As they drove, Katherine turned onto a side street in a lower middle-class neighborhood.

"Aren't we going home?" Nora inquired.

Ben and Carrie began to giggle as Katherine pulled up in front of a modest cottage with a one-car garage. She got out and

Nora and the kids followed. "What's going on?" Nora asked.

When they reached the front door, Katherine handed her sister a key.

Wonderingly, Nora inserted the key into the lock and opened the door. She gasped.

The children pushed past her into a living room furnished with second-hand but clean furniture. In the corner stood a Christmas tree, lights sparkling on the presents under it.

"What on earth?" Nora exclaimed.

"It's our new house!" Carrie shouted. "Come see my bedroom."

She tugged her mother down the hall, Ben and Katherine following. "See?" Carrie proudly showed her mother a small bedroom with a twin bed and a dresser.

From across the hall Ben called, "And here's mine."

Katherine led her sister into a slightly larger bedroom, with a queen bed and six-drawer dresser. "More comfortable than the van, I'll bet," she said.

Nora was dumbfounded. "This can't be ours!"

Katherine hugged her. "But it is."

Nora pulled away, frowning. "I told you I'd save up to get us a place. We don't take charity."

"This isn't charity," Katherine said as

the kids ran off to explore the presents under the tree, which she had placed there last night. "My bosses have contacts. This is a rental that the landlord agreed to lease to you at a minimum price. You don't have to have first, last, and deposit, like most places. You just have to pay the rent." She named a modest sum that caused Nora to smile. She added, "The furniture was donated."

They went back into the living room. "And this?" Nora gestured to the tree and presents.

"The kids and I went shopping yesterday," Katherine said. "They helped me set it up. We bought groceries, too. You're all ready to move in."

Nora threw her arms around her sister, tears damp on her face. "God surely led us to that Thanksgiving dinner—and back to you."

Katherine dabbed tears away with her fingers and said, "This calls for a toast. I'll be right back." She went into the kitchen and took a carton of eggnog out of the fridge Pouring four glasses, she set them on a tray and carried it to the living room, where Nora and the kids knelt in front of the tree.

She handed the glasses around and said, "Merry Christmas!" She lifted her glass and added, "Here's to your health, Norrie."

"And to your kindness," her sister replied, joining the toast.

Ben raised his glass. "Here's to Aunt

212

Katherine."

Carrie held hers up. "And to angels."

JOURNEY INTO CHRISTMAS

"Mom! Justin's tearing all my wrapping paper!"

"Am not! It's my paper, anyway!"

"Is not! Mom!"

Marilyn Beck leaned her forehead against the cool porcelain of the refrigerator, fighting back tears of anger and frustration. The thudding in her temples meant another miserable evening, and it wasn't yet three o'clock. Her stomach lurched in a way that had become uncomfortably familiar in the last few weeks.

The stretch between Thanksgiving and Christmas had turned into an orgy of arguments, accusations, and occasional fistfights between her children. Justin, Jamie, and Joelle turned from relatively nice children into hyperactive fiends who drove Marilyn crazy. Carols had been replaced by shouts of "Gimme!" and "I wanna." Christmas cheer had gone south, along with her sanity.

After a full day's work at the office, all she wanted to do was to plop on the couch. Instead she cooked, tried to keep the house clean, and refereed childish battles. She had no time to read stories or make decorations for the tree. Today, the day before Christmas, she had managed to start her holiday baking. And the kids had just derailed that undertaking.

She dropped an Alka-Seltzer into a glass of water and gulped it down, swallowing the gritty chunks instead of waiting for them to dissolve. Why couldn't the kids understand that everything was different now? With her husband gone three years, there weren't enough hours in the day for her to be the breadwinner, the housekeeper, and the mother. Surely they could make some effort to help her instead of constantly quarreling and making messes.

When Joel died, her life fell apart. Somehow she dealt with the aftermath of death, managed to find a job after years of being a stay-at-home mother, and tried to keep the routine of daily life somewhat normal. Lately it seemed like all she wanted to do was sleep. Yet she kept going. Her children depended on her, and she would not let them down.

In spite of her exhaustion this year, she bought a tree and wrestled it into the red and green stand, strung the lights she and Joel had bought the first year they were married, and hung the familiar ornaments. The kids gave her their Santa lists, but they changed their minds hourly. Marilyn tried to buy what they'd asked for and what she thought would be more than passing fancies. The insurance money had run out six months after Joel's death. Even with her income, she had to budget ruthlessly. She couldn't afford gifts that the kids would abandon an hour after they opened them.

To make this Christmas even grimmer, the winter was unusually cold and so far, there hadn't been even a flurry of snow. The kids hounded her, wanting to know when it would snow (the boys) and how Santa's sleigh would get to them if it didn't (her daughter), and refusing to play outside because it was boring (all of them). Chill wind blew through the yellow-brown grass and bare trees, and heavy clouds hung low over the land, refusing to spit out even a few flakes. The dampness and gloom had settled into her bones. A lifetime of white Christmases mocked her.

Her stomach settled, Marilyn went back to mixing the cookie dough, trying to concentrate on the spiritual side of Christmas, but the sounds of a life-and-death struggle erupted from the boys' room.

"Mom! Joelle's tryin' to peek!"

The sound of a slap cut through the shouts. Joelle shrieked.

Marilyn's control snapped. She stormed into the boys' bedroom and grabbed her six-year-old daughter by the arm. She shoved the terrified child into the hall. "Get out! I've had enough of your interfering!"

She turned on her eight- and eleven-year-old sons. "And you two! You're supposed to watch your sister, not beat her up. I'm sick and tired of you! I don't want to see you, I don't want to hear you! Just leave me alone!"

She charged out of the room, slamming the door behind her, blocking out the boys' stunned faces. Joelle cringed against the wall, folding into herself as Marilyn ran to her own bedroom.

She kicked the door shut and threw herself across the king-sized bed, sobbing and beating the mattress with clenched fists. Months of loneliness and anger poured out, carried on her despairing wails that rose higher and louder.

Through the fog of desperation, her mind whispered, *Stop it! You're scaring the children.*

Her dark side muttered, *Who cares? They deserve it.*

And finally: *Oh, God, just let me die. I can't do this anymore.*

She collapsed into semi-consciousness. Then sleep blotted out the horror of those uncontrolled minutes.

*****

The children huddled in front of her closed door. They had never seen their mother like this. Justin reached for the knob but the terrible stillness behind the door frightened him. His hand dropped to his side. Jamie and

218

Joelle looked at him, their eyes wide and scared.

"Mom was sure yellin'," Jamie whispered.

"She always yells," Justin whispered back.

Jamie swiped his sleeve across his eyes. "Not like that. I think she hates us!"

Justin opened his mouth to deny this, but the memory of his mother's distorted face kept him silent. Instead, he put his hands on his siblings' shoulders and guided them toward the living room. With Mom so far away, he would have to be the man of the house. *He* would have to keep them all safe.

Jamie collapsed on the couch and Joelle snuggled next to him, eyeing Justin, who stood helplessly in the middle of the room. The silence stretched out.

At last Joelle spoke. "Is Mommy gonna go away like Daddy?"

"'Course not," Jamie snorted. "Dad's dead. Mom's not dead, and she's not gonna die!" He spoke more to convince himself than to reassure his little sister. He had never told anyone that sometimes, when he woke in the night, he crept through the darkness to stand at his mother's bedside, as silent as midnight as he waited for a sign to prove that she hadn't died, too. Only after hearing her soft sleep-sigh or seeing the shadow-shape of her shoulder rise on an indrawn breath did he go back to bed, comforted that she was still there, protecting them.

Joelle slanted a look at him, unconvinced. She'd been only three when Daddy had died. She still wasn't sure what dead meant, except that Daddy went to sleep in a fancy box and he wouldn't wake up when she called to him, and when she asked her mother, "Why doesn't Daddy wake up?" her mother only held her tighter and cried some more. Maybe dead meant being away on a trip, and one day Daddy would come back and swing her high into the air and say, "How's my best girl?" It sure was a long trip, though.

Jamie worried at a hangnail as he said, "How come she did that, Justin? What'd we do?" He was genuinely puzzled. He didn't remember doing anything different today, except he didn't usually hit his sister, at least not that hard. Vague, but real, guilt overwhelmed him.

Justin flopped onto the couch beside Joelle. "Maybe she's just tired." He chewed at his lip as he thought about it. If he got cranky when he was tired, maybe Mom did, too. Thinking of Mom as a person made him squirm. She was supposed to be Mom, just Mom.

Joelle's lower lip trembled and a tear slipped down her cheek. "Will she still be tired when she comes out?"

"Naw. She's taking a nap. She'll feel better." Justin glanced around the living room. There must be some way he could hold them together, draw them away from the hurt and confusion their mother's outburst had caused. What would their father do?

Dad never lost his temper. He hardly ever yelled at them and he'd never spanked them. Justin tried to live up to his father's expectations. When Dad was alive, Justin kept his and Jamie's room clean, urging his brother to help instead of making him do it. He played with Joelle and taught her numbers and colors when she was little. And he'd watched Dad and Mom together, how they smiled and touched and were good to each other.

After Dad died, everything changed. Mom got so sad. Even when she tried to be happy and do the things they used to do, Justin knew it could never be the same. And that made him even sadder than losing Dad. He'd been sad and mad. If you couldn't count on your dad, who could you count on? He tried to be like Dad, to take care of Mom and the kids, but nothing he did seemed to help. Mom stayed sad and Jamie and Joelle wouldn't do what he told them.

And so he had given up trying to be like his father.

Mom's anger startled something in him that had been sleeping for a long time: empathy. Maybe he couldn't be just like Dad, but could he try to be a little more like he was when

Dad was alive? Could he be kind instead of crabby? Could he help instead of getting in the way when Mom or his brother or sister needed something?

Maybe, just maybe, he could bring back Dad's memory by the way he acted. And the idea sprang to life, an idea that would make Mom love them again.

He leaned close to the others. Excitement throbbed in his voice as he said, "You guys wanna surprise Mom?"

"Yeah!" Joelle clapped her hands.

"What can we do?" Jamie scowled at his brother.

"We could clean the house."

"The whole house?" Jamie was dubious; Joelle, uncomprehending.

"Most of it, anyway," Justin replied. "Lookit the mess in here. Joelle, your cereal bowl's still on the coffee table. And your p.j.'s are on the couch, Jamie."

Jamie refused to take the entire blame. "Oh, yeah? You got your Hot Wheels all over the floor!"

"I'm gonna pick 'em up. C'mon. Let's see how much we can get done before Mom wakes up. Let's have a contest. I'll keep score."

Justin whirled into action and the others followed. "Point for you, Jamie," he cried softly as his brother scooped up the dirty dishes from the coffee table. "And one for

222

me," as he tumbled the toy cars into their box. "Two for Joelle!" He giggled as she lay on her stomach and snagged a gaggle of comics from under the couch.

They scurried through the house, muffling their excitement while they flung armloads of clothes into the hamper and whisked their toys off to bedroom toy boxes. They put the dirty dishes into the dishwasher and dusted the furniture with an old flannel shirt. The smell of lemon polish mingled with the scent of Christmas tree.

And finally they were finished. Justin couldn't remember when he'd seen the house so clean. It looked like it used to before Mom had to find a job. And they had done it all by themselves. He grinned as he thought about how surprised Mom would be when she came out.

But Mom didn't come out. Justin put a finger to his lips and left the two sitting on the sofa as he tiptoed down the hall to Mom's bedroom. He put his ear to the door but could hear nothing. He reached for the knob but when he turned it the rattle scared him and he let it slip back into place. Maybe they should wait just a bit.

He tiptoed back to the living room. "We better let Mom alone for a little while longer," he said.

"But what if she doesn't come out?" Joelle's chin trembled as tears gathered.

223

Jamie scowled, but behind the frown Justin sensed fear. He had to keep them from thinking about Mom.

"Mom was making cookies before she...got mad," he said. He pasted a grin on his face and held out his hands. "Let's finish them."

Joelle and Jamie gaped at him. Cook *with* Mom, sure. But without her? Unthinkable.

Justin pulled them into the kitchen and rolled up his sleeves. He looked in the bowl on the counter. "See? They're all mixed up. All we have to do is cut 'em out and bake 'em."

He picked up the recipe card and read it slowly, aloud, to make sure he understood the directions. Jamie and Joelle moved closer. They poked at the molasses-spiced dough, fingered the shiny cutters, and ran their hands over the smooth aluminum trays.

Justin put down the card and dug a handful of shortening out of the can. As it splatted onto a cookie sheet, he said, "Joelle, you grease the pans. Jamie, you roll the dough out about this thick." He measured with his thumb and forefinger. "I'll turn on the oven."

Jamie dragged the stepstool from the laundry room and climbed up on it. He sprinkled flour on the counter, thumped the dough out of the bowl and began to roll it out. When it was just right, he pressed a star-shaped cookie cutter into the sweetness.

"I wanna do it." Joelle nudged him. Instead of shoving back, Jamie stepped down and helped her onto the stool. She grabbed a Santa cutter and went to work. Taking turns rolling and cutting, they filled the trays with bells and reindeer and Santas and stars.

Justin slid them into the oven and set the timer. The three hovered at the stove, peering through the oven window, waiting anxiously for that perfect moment called "done."

As each tray came out, Justin used a spatula to scoop the cookies onto wire cooling racks that Mom had already set out. Justin filled the cookie sheets again and again, until the last scraps of dough had been cut.

They worked quietly, intently. If they could do everything right, be good enough, then maybe their mother would come back to them.

*****

Marilyn woke, sluggish and exhausted from her tantrum. The awfulness of what she'd said to the children made her want to burrow back into the pillow and never leave her room. But something nudged her. She sat up, listening for little voices, for pattering feet, for the blare of the TV. Instead, there was silence.

Visions of runaways and other disasters flooded through her as she leapt off the bed and opened the door. She raced down the hall, only to stop as she entered the twilit living

225

room. She blinked. Surely the room hadn't looked this way two hours ago.

Soft murmurings and the aroma of baking came from the kitchen, drawing her to investigate. Tiptoeing to the doorway, she stopped, shocked. Plates overflowed with cookies. The dishwasher hummed quietly through its cycle. Joelle held the dustpan as Jamie swept crumbs into it. Justin was wiping the last traces of baking from the counter.

Marilyn's eyes misted and she swallowed hard. They were so young, so precious. She was all they had left. How could she have behaved so badly?

She crept to the tree and plugged in the lights, transforming the murk into a wonder of fairy lights and shining tinsel.

"Hey!" Three delighted children stopped short in the doorway, their faces lit with red, blue, green in the dusk.

"Mom! Hey! See what we did?" Three voices vied for attention. Six eyes sparkled. Three sets of fingers reached out, touching, stroking, loving Mom, who had come back.

Marilyn gathered them close, afraid to speak for the lump in her throat.

"C'mon, Mom." Butterfly touches guided her through the room, flung wide the door, led her out into Christmas Eve, where winter blossomed on hair, cheeks, and lashes.

"Hey, Mom! It's snowing."

An earlier version of this story appeared in *Grit* magazine, November 9, 1998.

A REAL ANGEL

It's not easy being an angel. Before I was one, I thought it would be, but I was wrong. See, if you become an angel when you're still a kid and not real well behaved, your bad habits come to heaven with you, and you have to show the Big Guy that you really can be good enough to be an angel before you get a gold halo instead of just a brass one like mine.

I don't care what that Clarence guy in the movie said, every angel gets a pair of wings as soon as he or she—there are girl angels, too, though I think they're too goody-goody—gets here. Well, maybe that's why girl angels have it easier than boy angels. 'Course, the wings are mostly for decoration. I mean, I don't have to flap them or anything to get around. I can just decide where I want to go and I sorta float there, fast or slow, however I want.

Anyway, when I was a kid instead of an angel, I had some bad habits. I wasn't patient. I didn't always mind my folks. And I teased my big brother something awful. Sometimes I snuck away and did stuff I wasn't supposed to do, like going down to the pond and throwing rocks to watch the fish jump.

Sometimes I even took off my clothes and went swimming. And in the winter I took my sled and coasted down the hill and out onto the ice. Mother kept telling me I'd be the death of her. Turns out I was the death of *me*.

I've been an angel for a long time. I was only nine when I became an angel in 1928. It was a cloudy, cold day in late November, and Sidney, my older brother, was off somewhere with his pals. He'd threatened to whip me good if I tried to follow them. Sometimes I hate being four years younger. But that's neither here nor there.

Anyway, I was moping around outside, trying to find something to do. If I sniffed hard, I could smell snow on the wind that nipped my ears, so when I decided to explore the pond, I ran back inside and took my brother's earmuffs. He probably wouldn't even miss them, 'cause I wasn't going to be gone that long. Just long enough to see if the ice was thick enough to skate on yet. If it was, I'd come home, grab my buckle-on blades and my own earmuffs (which were somewhere in the room I shared with Sidney), and come back.

By the time I ran the half mile to the pond, flakes were starting to swirl through the air, and I got even more excited. If the snow kept falling until tomorrow, I'd be able to sled down the hill and slide clear out to the middle of the pond before I stopped. If the ice was strong enough. Running made me hot, so I unbuttoned my heavy coat and flapped it to cool off.

The ice, darker gray than the sky, already had a thin coat of snow on it. I stepped out on it real careful. I slid my other foot forward. So far, so good. Another slide. Another. Before I knew it I was almost halfway across. Then the ice started to creak and groan, like ghosts crying. I turned to go back and heard the ice give a big crack. Before I could take another step, a hole opened and I dropped into the coldest water I'd ever felt.

Water filled my nose. I opened my eyes and saw the hole above me. My heavy ol' coat was soaked, my galoshes filled up and dragged me deeper. I shook my arms and bounced up a little as the coat fell off, but I couldn't get the galoshes off my feet. The hole got farther and farther away.

Well, I guess you don't need to hear about the last few minutes.

"Master Harold, where are you supposed to be?"

I jumped at the sound of St. Peter's deep voice. I swear that darned guy can be in sixteen places at once. That is, if Heaven allowed swearing. I looked up into his stern face. "Uh, I forget, sir."

He laid a hand on my shoulder. "Why do I not believe that?"

My eyes dropped. I might have been able to fool Mother and Father before I was an angel, at least some of the time, but nobody can fool the saints up here, especially St. Peter. He's in charge of letting people through the Pearly Gates and he can spot a faker quicker than anybody. I shrugged. "Well, sir, I guess I'm supposed to be on the corner cloud."

I sneaked a look at him. His long beard shook a little. He must be really mad at me.

"Then, Master Harold, I suggest you go to the corner cloud and stay there until the Father says it's all right for you to come back here."

"Yes, sir." I sighed and headed toward a cloud way over in the corner of Heaven. It's small and sad and that's where I spend a lot of time, thinking over the trouble that my bad habits have caused. Earlier the Big Guy caught me trying to slip back to Earth. I like to do that sometimes, just to look around. All of us angels can see what's happening all over the universe without ever leaving Heaven, but going back to my home makes me feel a little less lonely. See, that's one of the things about transitioning (a fancy word for dying). You can meet up with all your friends and relatives when they come over, but they're usually happy to just hang around, strumming harps and talking. Or maybe playing golf or bridge, if they're grownups. Not much fun for a kid who'd rather run and swim and have fun. I suppose someday I'll learn to be patient and do the right thing naturally instead of always having St. Peter or the Big Guy always telling me what to do. I know they're just trying to make me be better, but I really, really miss being a boy.

I could feel St. Peter watching me as I scuffed over to the corner cloud. I plunked down and sat with my elbows on my knees, my chin on my fists, staring down at Earth. I might have to keep out of mischief but I didn't have to like it. You'd think that the high mucky-mucks in Heaven might be a little forgiving, seeing as it's the season of goodwill toward men (does that include angels?) and the Big Guy's son was all about forgiveness. I settled in for a long, boring stretch of being good.

Hardly anybody comes to the corner cloud unless they're in trouble. I'd be all alone until the Big Guy decided to let me off the hook. St. Peter is always saying, "Master Harold, you can hear and see everything from Heaven. There is absolutely no reason for you to go down there."

Which is true. But eavesdropping isn't the same as being there. You sure can't play with real kids if you're stuck on some dumb cloud. But I guess I'll just have to be happy to eavesdrop. It's better than writing "I will

233

behave" a million times like I had to do a couple of decades ago.

I sighed and lay on my stomach, gazing down at Earth, wishing I hadn't gotten caught the last time. I had been just about to join some boys for a game of hide and seek when one of the lesser archangels showed up and dragged me back to heaven by my halo. It still has a little kink in it.

My old house is still there, but it's been changed and added to over the years and the city has edged out to the country, so it's only a couple of miles from the nearest neighbor instead of five, like it was back when I lived there. There's a nice family there now. They have a son who's almost a teenager and a younger daughter, as well as a couple of dogs and a cat. The boy's sister teases and torments him, just like I used to tease Sidney.

The day was darkening and big flakes drifted down. I could almost smell that cold, sharp smell that means winter and Christmas. I wished I dared go down and join the fun that was unfolding in a meadow about halfway between my old home and the pond.

Some friends of the boy, whose name is Josh, had come over to play and built two snow forts. They'd been there long enough for both sides to pile up a huge stock of snowball ammunition. There were three boys behind each barricade, still making snowballs. It looked like it would be an epic battle, kind of like the ones Sidney and I used to have when we were speaking to each other.

Sonja, Josh's sister, came running down the hill. "Hey, Josh! Can I play, too?"

Josh didn't even look at her. "Go on home. You're too little—and this is for boys only."

The other boys on his team snickered and rolled their eyes. "Dumb girls can't throw," one of them shouted at her.

Sonja scuffed through the snow that was almost as high as her knees and brushed off a stump that used to be a big walnut tree when I lived there. She sat down, put her chin in her hands, and gazed at the boys like they might change their minds if she concentrated hard enough.

The fight started! Snowballs zipped through the thickening snow, sometimes falling short, sometimes hitting an enemy square in the face. They screamed and yelled and their faces turned red from the cold and their struggles.

Sonja couldn't stand it anymore. She gathered up a double handful of snow and packed it into a ball, then ran toward Josh's side. Ducking behind the snow barrier, she popped up and threw the ball as hard as she could. It flew off to the side and splatted on the ground less than halfway to the other fort.

One of Josh's buddies shoved her out from behind the fort. "Get outta here, sissy girl."

Sonja fell right on her bottom and started to cry.

Josh shouted, "King's X!" and the snowballs quit flying. He lifted Sonja to her feet and snarled, "You're messing up the game. Go on home."

Sonja wiped her nose on her coat sleeve and said, "I'm gonna tell Mom and then you'll be sorry."

Josh gave her a disgusted look, then turned and called, "Game on!" Snowballs flew fast and furious.

Sonja, still sniveling, turned away and ran, only instead of heading up the hill toward home, she went the other way, toward the pond.

Uh-oh. I knew from my last visit, the one that got cut short, that the ice wasn't nearly strong enough to hold even a little girl if she ran out only partway. The middle was just slushy water. I stood up, cupped my hands to my mouth and shouted, "Sonja! Turn around!"

She slowed down, looking around like she might have heard me. Then she charged ahead.

I bit my fingernail (another bad habit they frown on up here) and paced the edge of the corner cloud. Somebody had to stop her before she fell in. The boys were still shouting and throwing ammo at each other. I ran to the other side of the cloud, looking for another angel or anybody who could go down and save her, but I couldn't see anybody. They must all be over by the throne room, getting ready to celebrate Jesus' birthday tomorrow. If somebody didn't do something right now, for the nice family below the day before Christmas would always be the day their little girl died. I shouted but no one heard me.

Okay, I was in enough trouble already, and I'd be punished if I disobeyed St. Peter's instruction to stay on the cloud corner, but I couldn't let Sonja run onto that ice. I didn't want another family to be as sad as my family was when I drowned. Plus, we already have way too many girl angels up here. We sure don't need one more.

I raced to the edge and dove off. In only a few seconds I was right behind Sonja. She had already run out onto the not-quite-frozen pond and was entering the danger zone. I zipped ahead and landed in front of her. She would have knocked me down if I'd been in a body. Instead, she saw me just in time to skid to a stop.

"Where the heck did you come from?" she asked. My wings and white robe didn't seem to bother her.

"You have to turn back, Sonja. Right now," I warned. "The ice won't hold you if you go any farther."

She looked around with wide eyes. Then she looked back at me. "How did you know my name?"

I moved toward her slowly, trying to ease her back toward thicker ice. She started to back up. "I just know, okay? I did the same thing a long, long time ago. Only I didn't have a guardian angel to warn me." I kept moving toward her. "The ice broke and I became an angel. So I know what I'm talking about. Turn around very slowly and tiptoe back to shore."

She spun around, ignoring my advice to go slowly, and started to run. The ice groaned and snapped. Icy water lapped around her feet.

"Oh, God!" I cried. Without thinking I grabbed her around the waist. I tried to rise up. I even used my wings for extra lift. We drifted toward the shore a few inches but the ice was breaking faster than I could fly.

Sonja screamed.

I grunted and strained. Suddenly I felt new strength, and in the blink of an eye we were back on solid ground. I dropped her and sat down beside her. She burst into tears.

I put an arm around her. "It's okay now. You're safe," I whispered. "Now go home and get dry and warm. And don't come down here again unless Josh or somebody is with you."

She sniffed and stood up. "You're an angel, aren't you?"

I nodded. "And I have to get back to

Heaven. They'll be looking for me." I must have looked pretty glum.

She said, "I hope you don't get in trouble for saving me."

I shrugged. "I've been in trouble before, but it was worth it. You'll go home to your family and have a great Christmas. So long."

And in an instant I was back on the cloud corner. Only it wasn't lonely now. Everybody in heaven, it seemed, had gathered around, including St. Peter and the Big Guy. Boy, I really was in trouble now, and they had all come to see me punished.

St. Peter took my hand and led me to where the Big Guy was standing. "Here he is, sir." He gave me a gentle push forward.

The Big Guy looked me over. "You were told to stay on your cloud, Harold. Why didn't you?"

Like he didn't see everything? Why was he asking me such a silly question? "I, uh, there was this girl, see..."

"Yes, I did see," he said. His voice was kind. "You saved a precious child."

Then the biggest surprise of all. Jesus stepped out of the crowd and took my hand. "Harold, you acted for the highest good, and for that—" He waved his hand over my head and I was suddenly covered in a soft, golden light. "You have earned your gold halo."

Everybody started clapping and I didn't

know where to look. Instead of being in trouble, I had gotten my dearest wish. But even better, Sonja and Josh and their family would be able to celebrate Christmas with joy.

I still have to sit on the corner cloud sometimes, but not nearly as often. Whenever I start to fall into my old habits, my halo shines a little brighter to remind me to be good. Maybe it won't be long before I remember all on my own.

The End

Jan Weeks is an award-winning freelance writer, journalist, editor, and proofreader. She teaches classes at Colorado Mesa University's Tilman Bishop Center that include *Creative Writing, Evil Editor Tells All, How to Submit Your Manuscript,* and *How to Write for Magazines.* She belongs to The Authors' Guild and Rocky Mountain Fiction Writers, and facilitates the Colorado West Writers' Workshop.

Her other books, *Season of Evil, Season of Dreams; Silverton Summer; The Secret of Spring Hollow;* and *The Centerville Code*, are available from Amazon. Her website is www.weeklit.com.

CPSIA information can be obtained
at www.ICGtesting.com
Printed in the USA
LVHW041840200819
628309LV00015B/1162/P